The Mark of the Artist

Artist

A Novel

~~~

By Gina M. Engman
~~~

First published in the United States of America by Gina M. Engman, 2024

ISBN: 979-8-218-64897-8

Cover design by Gina M. Engman

First Print Edition, 2025

For Walter—my Artist, my Love.

Chapter 1

The church bell tolled the hour—six brisk chimes rang across the town square. The white church steeple popped its head a bit above the low orange tiled rooftops of the tiny village.

Spring had finally come to this part of the country and all the window boxes were full of colorful tulips, daisies, and marigolds. Nasturtiums draped down from high windows and crept along sunny walls. A large rose bush blossomed in a wooden barrel in front of the Sow's Ear tavern. The tavern owner's wife planted it many years ago, though the bright pink roses did not quite match the clientele of an alehouse as the owner complained regularly, not that his wife cared two shakes what a bunch of ale-soaked rowdies thought of her beautiful delicate flowers.

The town began to wake. Wooden shutters swung open letting in the warm morning sunlight. At the bakery, sweet buns are laid on the windowsill to entice passers-by, the smell of sugar and lavender spreads across the square. Mr. Howard, the farmer, shouts at a group of boys who bolt in front of his wagon, heavily laden with the latest crop of beans and peas ready for market. The good children skip to school in blue caps and red checkered aprons, faces scrubbed and lunches tied in handkerchiefs.

The bells stirred pigeons and doves from their nests in eves of the church, so they flock together on the cobblestones of the square, shuffling around the fountain searching for their breakfast.

Sylvia watched the little birds from her seat at the fountain, tossing them bits and crumbs of the lavender bun.

Her sheep were done being watered, but morning brings such a bustle, one she never sees on the hillside with her sheep, that Sylvia lingered a moment on the fountain edge watching as more of the townsfolk stroll into town. A farmer's wife carried eggs to market while her friend gossiped about someone named Muriel. The two women laughed out loud as they passed the young shepherdess. A loud *Clang!* resounded through the square—the blacksmith starting his work.

Caroline, the town seamstress, opened her door and swept remnants of red thread onto the cobblestone street. Her dress was a magnificent emerald green with gold brocade, nothing like the shabby brown tunic and dingy white apron Sylvia wore. Caroline waved and called out to the farmer's wife. The women smiled and exchanged pleasantries. Then the seamstress turned back to enter her shop—her dress twirled around her, catching the sunlight and sparkling.

Something about the sight of the swirly green fabric made her sigh, so Sylvia stood and started to shuffle the sheep towards the north of town—out to the grazing fields of Mr. Albright, husband of the grand Mrs. Caroline Albright. Mr. Albright owned much of the land around the town, but has allowed Caroline to keep her shop since she loved it so much—at least that's what they told people. Truth was women from across the county come to buy dresses made by Mrs. Albright, allowing their husbands to pay a visit to Mr. Albright, making the couple quite rich. Funny what you learn being a part time housekeeper—and part time shepherdess.

Before Sylvia could get the sheep in order she noticed a bright cart bumping along the north road. The cherry-colored cart was drawn by an old mule, and sitting atop the driver's seat was a man with bright red hair. He was wearing a velvet green jacket and a matching top hat. The peddler circled the fountain slowly and finally stopped the cart near the bakery, where everyone must pass.

The peddler hopped deftly down from the driver's seat of the cherry-colored cart. He shuffled about and unfolded the side of the cart to display his wares. As the driver scurried about, a few of the townsfolk began to gather, whispering to one another about the strange red cart and the stranger man.

Before the whispering townsfolk could decide what to think, the peddler jumped up on a small platform and bellowed, "Good people! I, Javier Goodfellow, peddler of wonders, purveyor of parcels, spreader of trinkets, invite you all to peruse these wares. Behold!" He flicked his hand and a panel dropped on the right. Inside the hidden compartment was an onyx chest no more than a foot long and studded with rubies. "This once belonged to the Magistrate of Bulgaria. It is said to contain the writings of the Magistrate's chief wizard, but, alas, I have not had the courage to pry it open and see the wizard's writings myself." The peddler cast a downward glance and shook his long red hair.

"Good people!" he shouted again, looking up. "In the East, there is a magical land of gold and light called Shangri-La. There, in a castle of diamonds is a golden king who rules with a steady hand and a gracious countenance. Many people have searched for this fabled place and many more have lost their lives in that search. But I, Javier Goodfellow, have seen this land with my own eyes!"

The townsfolk squeezed in closer. The baker and blacksmith, who had been whispering near the rear, now moved to the front.

"After spending many nights in this glorious place, the Golden King sent me on my way and gave me this statue to remember my time in his kingdom." The peddler waved his hand and a panel on the left slipped away revealing a small golden statue of a chubby smiling man. The figure sat cross-legged and held his hands out to the side with fingers touching. *Ooo's* and *ahh's* murmured from the crowd.

"Ah yes, what an elegant king he was." Goodfellow nodded pensively.

The people broke into chattering as a man dressed in a bright green overcoat walked into the crowd. Murmurs of "Morning, Mr. Albright" chimed from the townsfolk, and the blacksmith stepped aside, allowing the man to pass to the front.

The peddler watched this obvious display of deference to the newcomer. The man was average height and going bald, which he tried to cover with a fluffy comb over. But his clothes were finely made and he had a gold chain strung from a pocket, which the peddler assumed went to a just as finely made golden watch. A younger woman in a fine green dress came to the balding man's side and he kissed her cheek. She was younger than him, but not enough to be a daughter.

"Good People!" Goodfellow called, grasping a golden rope. "Behind this curtain is perhaps the most enchanting item I've come across in my many years of travel. As I traveled through the mountains in Spain, I came across a band of gypsies who invited me into their camp. I was leery, for all know that gypsies cannot be trusted. But I was weary and in need of food, so I entered the gypsy camp. Around the fire the women danced—in a brazen manor, I tell you." He nodded to a group of elderly women who had gathered to hear this strange man's tale. "And the men played on pipes and lutes. As I watched the gypsy revelries, an old woman approached me. She took my hand and moved her finger on my palm." He spread his arm to the crowd in demonstration. "Her wizened face grew dim and she squinted. Then, just as quietly as she approached, she rose and drifted way in the darkness.

"In the morning, the gypsy band was gone, leaving nothing but the charred wood of the last night's fire. But in my hand is what you are about to see, good people." He paused and glanced side to side, eyeing the crowd. Then, *whoosh*! The curtain was pulled back and on a green velvet pillow was a ring of shining copper. Though small, the metal caught the morning sun and reflected it into the crowd. More *ooo's* and *ahh's* floated up from the townsfolk.

"I cannot say what this ring means, but surely the old gypsy woman left it because of its power. Why else would I wake to find it in the same palm she had read the night prior?"

The villagers nodded and agreed. Sylvia stood on tip-toe from the back of the crowd, but glanced back to her sheep when something yellow moved out the corner of her eye. The man in the green overcoat stroked his beard in affected contemplation.

"So come, good people, and see the other treasures Javier Goodfellow has to offer." The peddler jumped down from his platform and swiftly set up a table covered in the same green velvet, where he set out his trinkets. There was a ruby ring worn by the Count of Copenhagen before his beheading, for carousing with the mayor's daughter no less. He had a belt of woven brown leather once worn by a Roman centurion. Next was a large silver punchbowl marked with odd symbols Goodfellow found while trekking in the Alps. Though he could not confirm it, a goatherd told him it was the drinking goblet of a giant. The blacksmith paid forty-five for the bowl. He had whalebone dice won from stranded pirates that the tavern owner bought for ten, an ebony paintbrush Goodfellow bought from a monk in Italy, and a brass key said to unlock the door to Avalon, if it could ever be found.

The townsfolk bought dolls and tarnished utensils, satin pillows and leather-bound books. Goodfellow gladly told the origins of each item he sold, almost sad to part with them for such reasonable prices, but what is a traveling trader to do?

The man in the green waistcoat watched from the side as people made their purchases. "You, my good man, are wondering how much for the cloak," Goodfellow called out to him. The peddler motioned to a bright sea-green cloak hanging next to the ebony box of the Bulgarian Magistrate. The cloak had intricate gold brocade stitching, and the back was embroidered with a field of gold stars.

"You would like it for your…wife? The lovely young woman there." Goodfellow pointed to Caroline Albright who was perusing the wares with some of the local women.

"Quite right," Albright said in a low voice. "Her birthday is in two weeks."

"Well, if I may be so bold, sir, this cloak would be a wonderful addition to the lady's wardrobe. And for two-fifty it is quite a deal." Albright seemed unenthusiastic. "This cloak was worn by the Princess of Algiers when she rode her horse to meet her new bridegroom in Istanbul. And, I was told, it was blessed by a holy man to bring prosperity to her marriage.”

“Hmm,” Albright said in an obvious attempt to sound unimpressed, but Goodfellow saw he’d already made the sale.

“Tell you what, my good man, I will also part with this paintbrush along with the cloak. It was once used by a rogue master painter of the Florentine court.”

Albright picked up the brush. It was quite sturdy but felt lithe, and was carved with an intricate design of vines.

“Many ladies these days are learning to paint, I’m told,” Goodfellow added.

“Ah, not my Caroline,” Albright handed back the paintbrush. “My wife is a seamstress, quite talented, and enjoys that as her pastime—not that she needs to work, mind you.”

“No, of course, sir,” Goodfellow responded correctly. He laid the paintbrush next to a shiny oriental lamp and turned back to the other patrons. “That vase was sculpted in Greece, see the image of the dragon,” the peddler explained to the florist who had picked up the pearly white vase.

“Wait!” Albright called. He looked at the paintbrush and the cloak. “I will give you no more than one-fifty.”

Goodfellow laughed. “I’m sorry, my good man, but that is impossible. For the cloak alone I can go no lower than two hundred.” He turned back to the florist.

“I will give you two hundred but I want the paintbrush as

well," Albright said smugly. The peddler paused and glanced at the cloak.

"That, sir, is highway robbery. But as it will soon be your lady's birthday, I will do it for two."

"And the brush?"

"Yes, sir, and the brush." Goodfellow and Albright shook hands. "You strike a hard bargain, sir."

Albright smiled, pulling out his purse as the peddler wrapped up the cloak and brush.

By the time the noon bells rang across the square, Javier Goodfellow was five miles south of the town, his dead uncle's mule plodding along, cart bumping along the road, shipwreck-scavenged trinkets swinging back and forth from leather holders.

Chapter 2

The lush drapes were pulled open, flooding the grand ballroom of the Albright Manor with warm spring light. The maids busied themselves with sweeping and polishing. The smell of roasting meats mingled with sweet honey cakes in the kitchen. In the entryway, a grand crystal chandelier was lowered so the many crystal drops could be dusted and cleaned before the party.

Caroline Albright swept in from the drawing room, still holding her morning teacup and sighed overtly. Her dress was sage-colored and stitched with tiny red rosebuds along the hemline. Her hair was loose but fresh, no doubt ready for styling later in the night. She shook her head and squinted, scrutinizing the polishing job of one maid.

"Polish that table again." Mrs. Albright wagged her finger at a spindle-legged oak table. Her tone wasn't harsh, or even demanding, but that of a young woman plucked from the working class at twenty-two, who at twenty-eight could hardly remember what it was like to polish furniture. Though she still had her dress shop, it had been years since she made a dress from scratch without the aid of her assistant. Lucy made all the petticoats and did most of the embroidery now, with Caroline donning her silver thimble when clients arrived.

On top of the table was a tall white porcelain vase, an

arrangement of spring cuttings jutting out the top. Cherry branches with delicate pink blossoms were mixed with a few fuzzy cattails. There was a lone peacock feather with the cuttings, its golden eye flashing in the morning light.

"It simply won't do to have a dingy table with such a fine arrangement on top." Mrs. Albright moved a few of the cherry branches and a blossom fell off.

"Yes 'am." the maid bobbed and started polishing the table for the second time.

Mrs. Albright flitted off to inspect the rest of the house, but not before leaving her teacup on the nicely polished spindle-legged table.

That evening, the banquet hall of Albright Manor was swimming with fancy-dressed people. High society ladies had turned out in their finest ribbons and lace. Silver flatware reflected the abundance of candles on the three chandeliers hung over the lavish dining table. Clinking crystal tinkled in the background of loud conversation—most about how lovely the setting was for the lady of the celebration: Mrs. Caroline Albright.

Fresh spring flowers, tulips mostly, placed in fine crystal vases dotted the table with pink and yellow. The white china elephant Mr. Davenport and his wife Charlotte had given to Mrs. Albright for her birthday was placed in the center of the table and had sparked a flurry of conversation.

A maid in a grey dress, white apron, and tufted hat carried a large silver platter of whole roasted goose and root vegetables out of the kitchen. She danced around the corner and presented the platter for Mr. Albright's approval. He nodded to the maid and she placed the platter in the center of the long table, temporarily displacing the alabaster elephant.

"Mrs. Caroline Albright," the steward announced. The gentlemen stood and a gasp rose from the guests. Caroline floated into the banquet hall. Again, as was her style, she was wearing a daring emerald gown, counterpointed with intricate black and gold detailing along the bodice, wrists, and hemline.

But what stunned the most, and where the eyes of the guests lingered longest, was on a daring sea-green cloak tied at her neckline with twisted thick golden rope-ties.

Caroline Albright made her way down to her husband's seat where he stood and kissed her cheek.

"My darling. Happy birthday!"

"Thank you, darling."

"Happy birthday!" The guests charged their wine glasses. The gracious Mrs. Albright nodded about the room.

"Thank you. Thank you. Please everyone, sit, eat." The guests took their seats. Caroline turned to take her seat on the far end of the room, but noticed an empty chair next to Mr. Albright. She shook her head.

"He couldn't be here, even tonight?" she asked her husband through a stiff smile.

"He will. I'm sure he just lost track of the time."

Caroline gave an airy laugh. "And I'm sure the sounds of thirty people bustling about the house, not to mention the servants, went completely unnoticed?" Mr. Albright patted her hand, so Caroline took her seat.

The dinner moved along with courses of roasted pork and potatoes with butter. There was a lamb stew with fresh mint that received many compliments. Then fruits were served alongside baked honey cakes with fresh cream and almonds from Spain which Lord Hamilton had purchased on his travels. Many guests wished Caroline a happy birthday with a raised glass of wine. At one point Charles Lionel spilled a bit of au jus on the linen and his wife Sarah scolded him loudly, causing quite a scene, but all in all it was a perfectly lovely night.

The focus of conversation kept circling back to the wonderful green cloak Caroline had worn during her entrance. Now it was hung on a brass coat rack behind her seat, still in full view of the guests.

"Ah yes, it is lovely. Mr. Albright gave it to me for my birthday. It is so intricate, isn't it? The man who sold it said it was worn by the princess of Algiers to her wedding!" Caroline told Lord and Lady Hamilton, who glanced at each other ever so briefly with just the slightest of raised eyebrows.

"Why, how remarkable, Mrs. Albright," Lady Hamilton said.

"Sorry I'm late!" A loud voice called out from the doorway. A young man was walking very fast towards Mrs. Albright. He was wearing work pants like those of the servants, covered with blue splatter, and a mismatched grey jacket. His hair was damp, still dripping some in the back, and was obviously too long for a proper dinner party. He couldn't have been more than twenty-five.

"Happy birthday, stepmother." He came to her and kissed her hand. Caroline chuckled nervously.

"Thank you, Sebastian." She glanced at the splattered pants and saw people were whispering. Across the dining table Mr. Albright smiled wanly.

"I know I'm late, my apologies everyone," Sebastian gestured to the other guests. "But I had to put the finishing touches on your birthday gift."

"Oh, how sweet!" Lady Hamilton said. "What is it, Sebastian?"

He smiled. "Well, if everyone would follow me, and my lovely stepmother, into the entry hall, I will show you." He offered a hand to Caroline.

After a moment of indecision, she took her stepson's waiting hand.

"Of course, Sebastian."

The group followed the pair to the entry hall. Hanging on the wall was a fresh oil painting. Blue waves crashed on a sandy shore and gulls flew above the water. The greens and blues swirled and swam together in real contrast to the grainy shoreline. Bubbling seafoam lingered at the wave's crest and ocean spray created a translucent veil over the sand. The sky above was grey and the clouds arched across the waves like long fingers of steam.

"I remembered you mentioned to father how you wanted to see the ocean, so I thought I'd bring a bit of it to you, stepmother," Sebastian said. "Happy birthday."

Caroline stood stunned. All eyes turned to her. "Thank you, Sebastian."

"My boy, this is truly a masterpiece. I'd no idea Albright had such a talented son." Lord Hamilton clapped Sebastian on the shoulder. "Have you ever been to the sea?"

"Well no, sir. But I have seen sketches of beaches in a book once."

The guests began to whisper and Sebastian noticed Mr. and Mrs. Davenport were swaying slightly back and forth.

"It is as if I can smell the salt," one said.

"I know, I thought I heard a crash of a wave a moment ago."

"Ah, a bit too much cabernet, I think, George," another laughed.

"Well!" Caroline said, a bit louder than was normal for her.

"Shall we move to the parlor for coffee?" She turned and marched off.

Sebastian stood next to the painting, watching the dinner party guests slip away to the parlor. The silent waves crashed on.

~~~~~

Anna wiped her brow and accepted an ale from Sylvia. "I cannot believe how hot these damned hats are!" She swiped the poofy grey hat from her head. A mass of brown curls fell down to her shoulders. "How do you handle it?"

Sylvia shrugged. She'd worn hats her whole life so she didn't quite understand Anna's complaint. But there was quite a bit about Anna she didn't understand—like how she was fascinated by acorns, and how her skirt was of a fashion Sylvia had never seen, and how the songs she sang while she polished the silver could sound so lively yet so serious. She guessed it was because Anna wasn't from around here. "I guess you'd call me a gypsy," Anna had told her when they met two weeks ago. Oh, Sylvia had heard of gypsies from the other maids in the Albright household—they were thieves and practiced witchcraft. But Anna didn't seem evil, just strange.

"And why would a lady of the house want a *whole* goose set out on the table? It was looking at me when I served it."

"That's just how it's done."

Anna shrugged this time and took a gulp of ale. The two
~~~~~

servant girls were sitting on hay bales around a large bonfire set near three old oaks on the edge of the Albright estate. The trees cast intricate shadows and tall grass swayed at the edges of the light. The birthday dinner for Mrs. Albright had ended hours ago and the servants gathered now to unwind after so many days of extra work. Many of them had changed into their plain clothes, including Anna who was back in her favorite yellow skirt, but some still wore their serving uniforms. The cheering and singing were a welcome change from the two weeks of constant preparation for Mrs. Albright's dinner.

"So, Mr. Albright has no idea you do this? He does not notice the bonfire?" Anna pointed at the tall flames. For years, the servants of Albright Manor had gathered after dinner parties, balls, or other high society events at "Three Oaks." Sometimes people who did not even work for Albright would show up to join the festivities.

"If he does, he doesn't say anything." Sylvia sipped her ale. It was strong and uncut with water as she usually liked it. Anna had almost finished hers.

The two new friends sat watching the people move about the fire and enjoy one of the first warm nights of spring. Frosts were definitely over now, but foggy mornings were more than likely, Sylvia thought, thinking of tomorrow when she and Anna would take the sheep out to pasture. But at least it was warm now—warm enough for Lucy and Charles, Mr. Albright's driver, to slip away into the tall grass behind the furthest oak tree with a bolt of Mrs. Albright's best spun wool.

"Come ladies—let us dance!" called out a young man playing a violin. Sylvia's attention swung away from the romances of Mrs. Albright's assistant seamstress, and recognized the young fiddler as Henry the stable hand. She flushed and shook her head.

"I have my ale to finish, good sir," Anna taunted.

"Perhaps she doesn't know how." Henry goaded.

Anna laughed. "Well, I'd try if there was decent music playing." The other stable hands laughed and jeered.

"By all means, my lady." Henry handed her the fiddle.

Anna stood and dusted the straw from her skirt. Then she leaned her head back, finishing her ale in one long gulp. For a moment she looked at the fiddle, then smiled. She plucked a few strings then pulled the bow across them in one long steady note. The crowd of revelers all paused their conversations and turned towards her. She smiled again. "A-ya!" Anna called out and burst into a quick and lively dance tune. The others looked shocked for a moment, then joined in the dancing.

As Anna played the fiddle, she danced in a small circle near the fire. Her yellow skirt swished about and her curls bounced as her fingers flitted across the strings like finches on a clothes wire.

A rustle came from the tall grasses and a man joined the group from the darkness. At first a few servants thought Mr. Albright had finally become wise to their revelries. But when the man came closer to the bonfire they saw it was Sebastian.

"James, can you hand a man an ale?" His smile was only half and was more like a sneer to no one in particular.

Up stepped another bright young man, about the same age as Sebastian, with wavy blonde hair and an upturned collar. "Of course, sir."

"Oh, stop that shit, James, you know I hate it."

"Why do you think I said it?" James laughed and slammed an ale into Sebastian's hand. Sebastian laughed too, and drank half right there. James leaned against a hay bale, sticking a straw in his mouth. "Can I take it from your jolly tone that your father wasn't impressed with your gift?" James asked.

Sebastian swallowed the ale and laughed again, though this time it wasn't a pleasant chuckle—it was deep and slow, the kind one fears hearing in a dark alleyway at night. At the sound of Sebastian's angry laughter, some of the other men gathered around their master's son—the man they treated like a fortunate son inside the house, and a pub friend outside.

"My father," Sebastian growled. "Oh yes, he was very impressed. Impressed at my total arrogance." He took pull from his glass. "Says how dare I take attention from Caroline's—I mean my stepmother's—night. That now everyone at that pretentious party was talking about my painting and not about Caroline and her damn cloak he bought off that two-bit snake oil salesman. Like it really came from Algiers—they don't even have a princess!" he shouted. Many of the men grumbled about the stupidity of Mr. Albright, even though a few had also bought trinkets from Javier Goodfellow.

"Hey, I'm sorry, Sebastian," James said, handing him another glass of ale.

He shook his head. "I know, poor little rich man's son."

"No, I truly mean it. That painting was amazing. And people should rightly be impressed. It was like you could smell the salt."

Sebastian looked sideways at his friend, who just happened to also be his personal valet. "Thanks. Anyways, no more about that. Let's drink!" The men cheered and raised their glasses.

Sebastian finished his second ale and gazed across the bonfire's whipping flames. Violin music was playing and people were dancing. Sebastian squinted and noticed the fiddler wasn't Henry the stable hand as was normal, but a young woman. Through the flames her hair looked red and gold while she twirled and played a tune. Her yellow skirt spun out and almost caught the flames.

"Who's playing the fiddle?" he asked James.

"Henry."

"Didn't know Henry wore skirts. Maybe my lovely stepmother could make him a custom piece." Sebastian elbowed James and pointed at the young stable hand now kissing a pretty servant girl near the ale barrels. James looked towards the music and sniggered.

"Oh! I think her name is Anna. She's new, works with Sylvia in the fields with the sheep now that the dinner's done."

"Oh." Sebastian nodded.

James smiled, an eyebrow raised. "Why do you ask?"

"No reason. She plays well. I don't recognize that song."

"Nor do I, but it's lively. Speaking of Sylvia, I feel like dancing. Excuse me, *sir*." James bowed low to Sebastian, and went to take a turn around the bonfire with the young shepherdess. Sebastian stood laughing again.

Chapter 3

Life had returned to normal at the Albright estate. The silver was stowed away; the last of the wine had been drunk by the stable hands. All remnants of the Three Oaks bonfire were swept away by the rainstorm that blew up the next afternoon and lasted well into the night. The cinders dissolved much faster than the hangovers.

Mrs. Albright had returned early that morning to her dress shop. The green cloak from Mr. Albright hung proudly in the front window for all the town to see. She could be heard chirping away about her husband's gift at the bakery when she popped in to buy a lavender morning bun.

For Sylvia, it was back to the fields. The sheep were restless from being penned up and she could tell they were ready to jump around again. There would be plenty of new grass and clover for them to graze on after the storm. She woke with a smile when the rooster crowed at dawn, knowing that her days of dusting and polishing were at an end. Compared to her days in the fields, the past two weeks had been chaos.

"Things are so sweet here, so calm," Anna had told Sylvia while they scurried about the dining hall setting out the multitude of china plates and silver forks. Sylvia was too busy remembering which side the shrimp fork went on, and whether or not they were even serving shrimp, to realize how strange Anna's comment had been. Later, at Three Oaks, she asked what Anna had meant by calm. She'd shrugged and grabbed another ale.

At least now when Sylvia tromped about the fields after the rambunctious sheep she would have someone to talk to.

"Wear your boots. It'll be soggy, I'm figurin'," Sylvia told Anna while they dressed for the day. Anna put her walking stick down and rummaged through her large red carpet bag.

"Will these do?" She held up a ratty pair of shoes, one with a hole near the toe.

"Hmm," Sylvia scrunched up her face.

"I guess that would mean no. Do you happen to have a spare pair?"

"I wish."

"Well, then these'll have to do!" Anna chuckled and buckled up her shoes.

Sylvia got the impression some of the other servants didn't care for Anna—it's easy to hear whispers when people think you're invisible. At first Sylvia thought it was because Anna asked too many questions, but she wasn't finding fault with how the linens were folded or questioning the cook's skill when he added hazelnuts to a pork stew. Anna just wondered why.

Then she figured it was because Anna danced and played the fiddle at Three Oaks. "Just like a stable hand," one of the older maids had scoffed—though how she knew about Anna's playing Sylvia wasn't sure, the older woman hadn't even been there. Funny, if the Master's son didn't find fault with her, then why should the old maid care?

The women set out for the western fields of the Albright land. Spring grasses were thigh high and holding tightly to the rain of the night before. Violets were beginning to spread a deep purple carpet under the trees.

"Look at all the royal thyme, Sylvia." Anna pointed to the deep purple and yellow flowers.

"The what?" Sylvia asked, tapping a stray sheep on the hindquarters with her shepherd's crook.

"Royal thyme."

Sylvia followed Anna's finger. "You mean 'violets?'"

"Oh…yes, I guess. My Grandad called them royal thyme." Anna looked over the western hills.

"Well, I heard them called 'Johnny-jump-ups' before, but never royal thyme." Sylvia bent and plucked a few of the blossoms. Anna nodded absently. Her expression changed in a flash from sad detachment to concern. "Is that one of our sheep?"

"Oh no! Come on!" Sylvia took off running up a steep embankment, whistling at the wandering sheep. Anna hitched up her skirts and sprinted after her like a jackrabbit.

The sheep had paused at the top of a drop-off to munch the new violets sprung under a weeping willow. Just the other side of the hill was a stream. Swelled with yesterday's storm, Anna heard its current crashing over the rocks.

Sylvia finally reached the top of the embankment and reached out for the sheep, trying not to startle it.

"Come on, Tilly." she stretched out her hand. "It's okay, let's go back, you silly sheep." Sylvia laughed. "Anna, this one you'll have to watch. Tilly likes to—"

Sylvia's footing went out from under her as the softened mud slipped down the hillside. Anna caught up just as Sylvia fell down hard on her backside.

"My foot!" Sylvia cried out. Tilly skittered, and the wayward sheep scampered off back to the herd.

"Don't move," Anna said as she knelt down next to the injured shepherdess. "Let me see it." With such quick movement, Anna removed Sylvia's boot and looked at the swelling ankle. "It's not your foot, it's your ankle. Can you move it?" Sylvia tried moving her ankle in a slow circle and though she winced, it moved with a full range of motion.

"I think it is just twisted," Anna said. "You'll be able to walk. But let's rest it for now." Anna glanced around her. "Damn, I dropped my walking stick. Fine, we'll sit under this tree for a bit." Anna pulled Sylvia up and the two limped over to the willow.

The rushing water from the stream below crashed and babbled over polished rocks. The willow bent down low and many of its leaves floated on the surface of the water.

"My lord this hurts," Sylvia exclaimed, putting too much weight on her foot.

"That's why I said to sit for a bit." She helped Sylvia to a sunny spot on the ground, then stretched her own foot as she sat down next to her.

Sylvia furrowed her brow. "Did you break your ankle sometime?" Sylvia rubbed hers and winced.

"No, my foot."

~~~~~~

The air was salty. Waves crashed, and above a gull screeched, echoing and hollow. Her hair was matted and tangled in her face, smelling of sea water and sand. Her heartbeat was in her ears, thumping hard inside her head.

Wispy grass leaned down against her bare arms when a gust blew by.

There was sand in her nose, so she snorted, but it didn't help.

The sounds were loud and yet muted somehow. They echoed—the waves, the gulls, and the small voice calling, "Senorita?"

Anna opened her eyes and the dull grey of early dawn pierced her eyes, matching the raw pain radiating from her head and left foot.

"Hmm…" Anna responded.
~~~~~~

"Estás bien, Señorita?"

"What? I don't…Where am I?"

"Oh, you are English. Miss, please are you hurt? Here, drink some water."

A small tin cup was placed to her lips. Cold water with the tang of minerals spilled out and Anna gulped it down.

"Oh my head!" she said, putting a hand to her temple.

"It is from lack of fresh water, miss." Anna opened her eyes wider and saw three young women looking down at her.

"Can you sit up?" one woman asked and helped Anna to a sitting position. Anna's head was swimming and she grabbed the young woman's arm to steady herself. The young woman's tunic was made of rough woven grey wool. All three of the women wore matching garments and head coverings. Anna squinted then nodded her head.

"Thank you, sisters."

"Of course, miss," the first nun responded. "I am Sister Maria Novella. And this is Sisters Gloria and Rafaela."

"Annalisa Lenore."

"Pleased to meet you." Sister Maria turned to the others and spoke in a language Anna didn't understand.

"Where am I? Last thing I remember, Captain Clark was laughing at me from a rowboat." Anna rubbed her eyes. She looked behind her and saw the ocean roaring down below. It was grey in the morning light, white caps forming in the gusty wind. She was on a low bluff overlooking the ocean. It must have been low tide since lines of seaweed were running along the sand marking the range of the high tide's reach. The bluff rose a few yards above the sandy dunes, but sand covered the reddish ground. To her right she noticed a protruding stone circle with a bucket nearby—a well, perhaps from a natural spring.

Anna turned back to the sisters. Sister Gloria was kneeling near her feet, talking quickly with Sister Rafaela and reaching out for a stick and cloth strips. But Sister Maria held the cup to her lips again and Anna sipped more water.

"You are in Colina Roja. Spain," Sister Maria said, her eyebrows raised, hoping for a glimmer of familiarity. "Where were you going?"

Anna rubbed her temples again. "Well…I don't think it was…Spain." She closed her eyes. "No, I was going to see family…in…" Anna struggled to remember.

The sisters glanced at each other and began speaking again in the other language. Anna looked around and saw her red carpet bag a few feet off, so she stood to retrieve it. But as she pushed herself up she stumbled, blinding pain shot up her left leg from her foot and she screamed.

"Oh no! Do not stand, miss." Sister Maria put a hand on Anna' s arm and helped her back to the sandy ground. "Your foot, I am sorry, it is broken.”

Anna again felt the raw pain in her left foot that had been overshadowed by her headache and thirst. She looked down. Either she had lost her shoe somewhere on the beach, or one of the nuns had removed it. Her foot was swollen and turning a dark blue.

“We were about to bind it when you awoke. Sister Gloria is a great healer.”

Anna was breathing hard and her head began to swim again.

“We will take you to the abbey so you can rest, Miss Annalisa.”

~~~~~

Sylvia’s head was tilted when Anna looked up at her.

“How’s your ankle?”

“Oh,” Sylvia shook her head. She stretched out her leg and moved her foot in a small circle. “It hurts, but I guess it’s not too bad.”

“Well, we should probably get you up to the house in case it swells too much. And I’ll get the sheep. Give me your hand.” Anna smiled.

As Anna and Sylvia limped back to the house, trying not to scatter the sheep as they went, James and some of the other servants were busy under the watchful eyes of Mr. Albright. The men had spent much of the morning on ladders in the entry hall with
~~~~~

hammers. Now they were again on their ladders, this time in the third floor guest room. Dust floated up and many of them paused in their work to sneeze, careful not to drop a hammer on their fellow servants.

"Never mind, that's fine there, men." Mr. Albright cocked his head to the right, shrugged, then left the room. The men picked up their tools and went back to their work elsewhere.

James picked up the last ladder and shook his head. Henry, who had been called in from the stables to help with Mr. Albright's project, grabbed the other end. "I know what you're thinking, James," he said.

"I'm not thinking anything."

Henry watched one of the other stable hands leave the room. "I agree. Sebastian is going to be pissed as hell."

No sooner had the words slipped from his mouth than they heard Sebastian shouting from downstairs.

"Father!" Sebastian yelled. He was in his work pants, splattered in black paint, and his hair was skewed on one side. The white shirt he wore was untucked and spots of blue paint covered his left arm. But the wildness of his clothing was not nearly as crazed as the look on Sebastian's face. There was a mix of confusion and rage that James had only seen once before: when Mr. Albright had told the young man his mother had been taken by the water sickness seven years ago.

"Father, where is it?" Sebastian yelled. Mr. Albright entered the entry hall from his study. Sebastian saw some of the servants peaking around the corners and doorways, eager to see what the master's son was up to this time.

"Son, please calm down." Mr. Albright glanced around at the door to the kitchen and a maid ducked out of sight, but not out of earshot.

"Where the hell is it?" Sebastian pointed to the empty place on the wall of the entry hall where his painting for Caroline had been hanging that morning when he went into town. In its place was a low table with the cream colored elephant Mr. and Mrs. Davenport had given Caroline at her party.

"Well, son, I had it moved."

Sebastian glared. "Where?"

"The third floor guest room."

"Are you kidding me?" he yelled. "That dust covered hole?"

"Now Sebastian, be reasonable."

"Reasonable? Reasonable. Father, do you realize I worked on that painting for Caroline for two months?"

"*Stepmother.*"

"What?" Sebastian growled at his father.

"You mean *stepmother*. You need to show some respect for her," Mr. Albright said to his son, a hint of regret already in his voice.

"I should—" Sebastian took a deep breath. "You think I

should have more respect for a woman who is only ten years older than me? A woman who spends her days concerned for clothing and dresses?"

"That is her profession, son. She's a seamstress." Mr. Albright stood up tall and smiled proudly.

"She doesn't even make those things! If it wasn't for her assistant, nothing would ever get made at that damn shop!"

"Now you watch what you are saying about your mother, Sebastian," Mr. Albright yelled.

Sebastian became very quiet. "Caroline is not my mother." Sebastian's face was very dark, and his fists began to tremble. "Or have you forgotten that already, father?"

Mr. Albright swallowed hard. "No, of course not, Sebastian."

The two men stared at each other for a moment. Sebastian took another deep breath and rubbed his forehead. "Well, it is good to know I'm not the only one who remembers my mother." He glanced back at the empty wall. "So, father, do you mind telling me why you decided to move my gift to my *stepmother*, and replace it with that, that porcelain lump?"

Mr. Albright hesitated. "Well, the fact is that Caroline wasn't too fond of the painting. So I—"

"You must be kidding me! It was a gift. Does that mean nothing to that shallow idiot?" Sebastian's eyes were narrow and his fists clenched tighter.

"That is enough!" Mr. Albright boomed. "Now, I am the master of this house, and if I decide something, then that is that," he rambled out his standard response.

"Funny, I thought you said Caroline—pardon, I mean my *stepmother*—decided it?" Sebastian pushed past his father and stomped out to his workshop.

"What are you going to do, sir?" James asked as he ran to follow him.

"If Caroline doesn't appreciate the work I went to to make her that painting, then she doesn't deserve it." Sebastian slammed the wooden door of his shop open, grabbed a can of paint and tromped off back to the house.

In the third floor guest room, the painting leaned against the back wall. The waves crashed on in silence, the spray shooting up and the gulls crying out. Sebastian stood staring at the painting, a can of black paint in one hand, the other balled up tight. It was as if he couldn't decide whether to throw the paint or the fist.

"Sir, do you really want to ruin it?" James asked, out of breath from running up three flights of stairs. But Sebastian didn't answer. He stared at his painting. His look was far away, lost. Slowly he set the paint can on the wooden floor. From the back pocket of his paint splattered pants he pulled the carved paintbrush Mr. Albright had given him.

Sebastian dipped the brush in the black paint, carefully

flicked off the extra, right onto the dust covered walnut hardwood floor, and grabbed a stool. He stood so still.

Then with such careful, deliberate motions, Sebastian reached out and began to paint.

After half an hour Sebastian got down off the stool. He stood back and James joined him.

"Why did you add that?" James asked.

"It just felt right, like it was missing something."

"But why is it sailing away from the coast? You can barely see its sails."

Sebastian shrugged. "Don't know."

Chapter 4

Anna sat up awake in her room thinking of the ship. How the spray of the sea soaked her to the bone when they shoved her out of the rowboat and into the surf.

"You're lucky I'm a compassionate man, missy," the ship's captain had called after her as she sat in the foaming surf. "If you weren't a lass, I'd have tossed you in the sea. No one stows away on the *Black Eel!*" The captain with his crooked eyes laughed and the rowers joined him. Anna had tried to stand up in the waves but stumbled. She kept her gaze set on the captain as they rowed back to the black ship. But she couldn't figure out why they were calling the ship the *Black Eel*. That morning she'd been walking the deck of the *Pegasus*, talking kindly to the Captain, a tall man with a red mustache, not this evil one she was staring at now. There had been fresh salt air in her hair, and a black storm on the horizon. She'd seen lightning far off...or had it been closer?

Once she could no longer see the rowboat, she turned and staggered up the beach to the rocks, limping on her one good foot through the mucky sand.

Sylvia moaned in her sleep and Anna broke from her memory. The clock in the hallway of the Albright servant quarters was striking eleven. Outside the night was quiet—no wind pounded the Albright home, there was no moving on.

Sylvia's ankle swelled up that night, and the next day Mrs. Horton, the head housekeeper, put her on kitchen duty—washing pans while sitting on a stool and peeling potatoes and turnips for dinner.

"If you and that gypsy girl had taken better care, the sheep wouldn't have to spend all day penned up. You know how Mrs. Albright wants the sheep fed on wild grass so their wool will be perfect for her clothes," Mrs. Horton scolded. With Sylvia limping about the kitchen, and the thought of angering Mrs. Albright, Mrs. Horton had no choice but to send Anna to graze the sheep.

"You'll have to keep an eye on Cappy, she's the one with a grey tail. She likes to lag behind the flock. And then there's Cranberry—she's the one with black patches on her hindquarters. Cranberry will nip at your fingers if you're not careful. Oh, and of course there's Tilly—you know what kind of trouble she can be!" Sylvia pouted in their room.

"I will take great care of your sheep, Sylvia. And you'll get a full report each night, I promise." Anna reassured her.

The sheep were quite lively once Anna led them to the Albright grazing fields. The violets bloomed and the grass swayed in the breeze. Everything seemed so perfect. Anna felt a calm and peace she'd not felt since hobbling around the convent gardens with Sister Maria. The gardens of the abbey had held carefully tended herbs and vegetables, and here the flowers sprung up at random, but both places put a sense of serenity in Anna. She took a deep breath of the fresh air and sighed.

Soon Anna found herself hiking up the steep hill, herding the sheep along with her. She stopped next to the weeping willow where Sylvia had fallen. Curious to see the stream, Anna stepped close to the edge of the drop-off. The embankment was nearly ten feet high—much taller than she had noticed when dealing with Sylvia's ankle. Down below, the waters were running fast with winter run-off.

"Tilly!" Anna called. The wandering sheep was taking a long drink from the stream. "How'd you get down there, you silly sheep?"

She glanced around and just on the other side of the willow Anna spotted a rough trail leading down to the bank of the stream. But perhaps trail was too good a description—it was really nothing more than a spot where the grass had been stomped down by someone walking.

"Come on little sheep!" Anna persuaded the rest of the small herd down the footpath. Once the sheep reached the bank they scattered to the edge of the water to drink. Anna joined them, laying her walking stick on the smooth stones and sipping from her cupped hands.

While the sheep were occupied drinking from the rushing stream, Anna strolled along the bank. Cattails grew in clumps surrounded by rushes and thistle. She spotted a beaver dam not far off, and a mallard swimming in a shallow inlet. From above, the weeping willow's branches curved over the side of the hill, leaves floating along the stream. The stream flowed very close to the hillside at this point, so Anna reached out and swept the willow branches aside to continue her walk along the water.

Behind the drooping branches was a large opening in the hillside—not a true cave, per se, but a small hollow just tall enough for Anna to walk in. The walls of the cave looked like stone, much like a mineshaft. But as she turned back to see the opening again, she saw they were covered in swirling patterns. Anna took her walking stick and propped the willow branches out of the way, allowing the mid-morning light to filter into the cave.

She crept further into the hollow. At the opening, the paintings were bold and geometric, very innocent. Many were animals and birds, ducks floating in the rushes, cows and sheep. For a moment Anna thought these paintings were made by those people of long-ago who dwelled in the caves and discovered fire. But after a few more steps, she saw a wagon being pulled by a horse and changed her mind.

As Anna went further into the cave the light began to dim and the paintings took on an almost blue glow like water after the sun has set. She moved closer to the side of the hollow, squinting to make out the next image on the wall, when all the light went out.

She spun around and realized there was someone else in the cave. This person was much taller than she, or at least his shadow made him seem so. Whoever it was had kicked her walking stick out of place and sent the willow branches swinging back into their normal spot.

"Who goes there?" Anna called, her voice echoing against the cave walls.

"Who asks?" a male voice returned.

Anna paused. "I asked you first."

From outside she could hear the gurgling and rush of the stream and, every now and then, the bleating of one of the Albright sheep.

"Get out of my cave," the man responded. It never occurred to Anna that an animal might be using the cave as a den; it turns out there was a human using it as such.

"Why?" she asked.

The voice sighed. Frustration, Anna could tell.

"Are you the one who did the paintings?" Anna saw the figure stoop down. The smell of matches hit her nose a second before the lamp glowed to life. The man holding the lamp was very tall, as Anna had suspected from his shadow. His dark hair was in disarray and he had paint on his white shirt.

"What are you doing here?" he asked. "Just get out." At the man's feet was a wooden box with drips of red and yellow paint on the outside.

With more light, Anna looked around the walls of the cave.

Even the ceiling was painted—images of the sun and stars, the moon at all its phases, sailed across the false sky. Along the left side, the painter had made a stream to match the real one outside. River otters popped their heads out, and moles dug their hills. An eagle perched on a sparse pine tree branch. Along the other side of the cave, an ocean crashed. Anna saw the figures of shells, and ships, and fishing nets, of walruses and wings. Not to mention the intricacy of the beautiful waves.

Anna had heard the night before about all the ruckus between Mr. Albright and his son over a painting of the sea. According to Allegra, a kitchen maid who saw the whole thing from around a corner, Mr. Albright had taken down the painting the son had made for the lady of the house's birthday. Anna heard that the son had quite the temper.

"Are you just going to stand there, or are ya gonna kick it?" The man hitched his thumb over his shoulder. The raised voice snapped Anna back to the present.

"Of course, Master Albright. Please pardon me for intruding upon your cave and admiring your lovely work." Anna curtsied low.

"Oh for the love of God!" he yelled. "Don't call me that!"

"What, Master Albright?" Anna asked.

"That!"

Anna stared at him. Sylvia had said to call the elder Albright sir or Mr., his wife ma'am or Mrs. and the son either sir or master.

"I don't understand, sir."

"Just…just get out." He hitched his thumb again. Anna walked slowly past the young painter. He kept his gaze on the wall of the cave as she passed.

At the entrance of the painter's cave, Anna paused and turned back to him. "You are quite talented. Not many could paint waves with such beauty without ever having seen the ocean." She picked up her walking stick and marched to find Sylvia's sheep.

As she walked up the footpath, whistling for the herd, the sound of crunching footsteps chased after her.

"Hold there!" the young painter called. "Wait, how did you know I've never seen the ocean?" He grabbed her arm and pulled Anna to face him. She yanked her arm out of his grip and cocked her fist, a total reflex, and Sebastian raised up his hands in embarrassment. Not sure if she should continue, Anna stood staring at him again. "Please, miss, tell me."

"A fellow maid who served at Mrs. Albright's dinner party overheard one of the guests ask you, sir."

"Sebastian," he said and smiled. "Please, don't call me 'sir.'"

Anna laughed, realizing she would still have her job tomorrow.

"Are you the girl who played the fiddle at Three Oaks the night of Caroline's party?" Sebastian asked, smiling a bit now too. "I recognize you now that the sun is on your hair." He coughed and tried to act like he hadn't just said something about the young woman's hair before even knowing her name. Anna chuckled.

"Annalisa, but you may call me Anna."

"Pleasure," Sebastian said.

They stood in the tall grass at the top of the embankment, the only sound the gurgling stream and more sheep bleating.

"Tell me, Sebastian," Anna said, breaking the silence. "How does such a talented painter of the sea become so skilled at drawing courtesans?"

Sebastian's jaw dropped open and he stuttered to say something. Anna laughed out loud. "It is hard not to notice the girls with wild skirts when they are painted next to a scene of seagulls lighting on rocks!"

"I never thought anyone would see any of those," Sebastian finally spit out, turning the color of a rutabaga. "It was a joke for James' birthday. Do you know James? He's my valet." Sebastian was talking very fast.

"Please do not worry, I have seen much worse." Anna laughed and resumed calling for the sheep.

Chapter 5

Rumors spread throughout the Albright household that the new gypsy girl had confronted Master Sebastian in the fields. Clara heard she had insulted his artwork. A stable hand heard the girl had spat on the young master and called him ungrateful. Henry told Sylvia that the gypsy girl—"Anna," Sylvia corrected him—had placed a gypsy curse on all of Sebastian's paints.

Sylvia did not know if Anna could place curses or not, but she cursed her own bad luck at missing the whole to do while sitting on a stool peeling potatoes in the kitchen. And the next day looked like another riveting day of kitchen duty since the swelling in her ankle had not gone down. Anna had said it could take a week or more and she should just be thankful it was not worse. She had made a poultice of herbs to speed her healing, but that was far from a curse, Sylvia guessed.

Once Sylvia was settled in the kitchen, Anna left in the early morning light with the sheep for another day in the fields, away from the rumors and whispers.

A few minutes later, James went to the workshop and found its owner missing.

Sebastian and Anna sat on a large boulder near the stream. Oddly enough, he had been taking a stroll in the western fields when Anna brought the sheep to graze. So he showed her the spot just downstream of his cave where the large boulder jutted into the stream and the spring runoff moved the current, swirling 'round the rushes. Many evenings he would come to this spot, looking over the water and the oaks and waving grass, and watch the sun set on his father's land, he told her. He liked to paint here too. His favorite time, he said, was in late August when nightfall brings a grey hush and the heat of the day's sunrays radiate back from the stone. Then again, the blue shades of pre-dawn in early fall were an inspiration for the blues of the waves in Caroline's painting.

"The sisters were so good to me," Anna told him. "They took me in after washing up on shore and they healed my foot. You should have seen it, it was as deep a purple as the royal thyme, erm, I mean *violets*."

"Ugh, sounds great." Sebastian winced at her description of the mangled foot. "Is that where you got that?" He pointed to her walking stick.

"Yes, it was a gift from Sister Maria." Anna showed him the intricate carvings on the polished wood. Christian symbols were woven together with a vine that spiraled around the stick. "This one"—she pointed to a large tree—"is a symbol of St. Christopher, the patron of travelers." Anna turned away and looked to the west.

"It's really good, very skillfully made, I'd reckon," Sebastian remarked. "So, you never told me: where did you see things that were worse than those, you know, things I, uh…"

"Courtesans?" Anna laughed at Sebastian's struggles.

He sighed and examined the stone quite thoroughly. "Yeah."

Anna stifled another laugh, but a grin played about the corners of her mouth. "In Spain."

"At a convent?" Sebastian sat upright, the look of disbelief was comical.

"Of course not!"

"Oh well, you said Spain and you told me about the convent, so I…"

Anna just shook her head at the young man who only two days before had been but the son of her employer.

~~~~~

Señora Elena handed Anna her money from the night—it wasn't a bad haul, considering how watered down the ale was, but no one seemed to notice. With so many ships in the port this week, Señora Elena's boarding house and cantina had been very busy. The sailors and traders spent their time making deals and drinking ale. When the deals went well, the traders became more generous, leaving extra coins on the tables. When the deals went bad, they would drink more ale, also leaving more coins on the table.

Though she had only worked for Señora Elena for about a month since departing Colina Roja and the sisters at the abbey, Anna had been able to stash away quite a bit. Hopefully in another month
~~~~~

or so she would have enough to buy passage to the place called England. Sister Maria had told her to go to England, since Anna spoke English, but Anna had never heard of such a place. Hopefully it wasn't too far.

Pepita shuffled down the back stairwell carrying a purple velvet bag. She was pulling the cords tight, but Anna saw the shimmer of her black heels when they caught the lamp light. Her hair was pinned up in a bun, but a few stray curls fell at her right temple where a red rose was placed earlier that evening. Pepita's black lace fan swung from her wrist as she scurried passed the bar.

"Adios, amigas," she called to Señora Elena and Anna, but she was barely audible over the woops and whistles of the patrons. Pepita paused at the door and spun around, her multi-colored skirts spinning with her. She bent slightly and blew a kiss in the men's direction, sparking more cat-calls. She just as quickly spun herself around and was gone.

"Senorita! Una más," a loud sailor barked. Anna slipped her coin purse into a pocket and picked up another mug of ale. She dropped it on the table in front of him.

"Es cuatro," she said. Since her time in the abbey she'd acquired only enough of this language to get by, and just barely.

The sailor grinned revealing the beginnings of scurvy, his gums bleeding, painting his few teeth a shade of watery red. The sailor said something to her she couldn't understand, so she simply repeated herself. Apparently he was requesting to pay for his ale in a way other than with coins, because he grabbed her backside. That was when he hit the floor.

"No, señor." Anna loomed over the drunken sailor—the walking stick from the sisters firmly in her left hand. "Ahora es diaz."

The sailor's compatriots sat laughing at their mate as he handed her the proper amount of coins.

"Good night, Anna," Señora Elena told her after they kicked out Anna's would-be patron and his shipmates. "I would say you have done enough for one night."

She nodded and picked up her red carpet bag from behind the bar. "Are you sure? There are still a few left." Anna surveyed the tavern. A couple of sailors had passed out in the corner, and the rest of the tavern folk looked like they would soon follow suit.

"I believe I can handle it." She winked. Not many people would hire a girl off the streets and give her a room, but with Mother Superior's blessing Señora Elena happily opened her cantina to Anna. Señora Elena, who was about fifty but moved like a young dancer, had spent her own time at the Colina Roja abbey. All others had turned away the ragged, unmarried dancer and her infant daughter, but the sisters had not, all those years ago. "Give Brother Laurentino my best, Anna." Señora Elena pressed two coins into her hand and floated off to serve more ale.

"Buenas noches, Señora Elena. I will return to my room soon," Anna called as she walked out the back door of Elena's tavern.

The drizzle was thick and almost fog-like as she walked the cobbled streets to San Judas Tadeo's parish. Brother Laurentino kept the fire burning late in the rectory on the nights before he trekked out to the monasteries and abbeys, bringing the sisters and other friars alms and supplies and news of the city's faithful and not-so-faithful. With half her coins from the night stashed away for travel, Anna envisioned the bread and plant seeds the rest would buy for Sister Maria and the others. Perhaps more wood so they could continue to create works of art like her walking stick or the holy icons on the walls of the abbey.

As she drifted back from the images of the serene chapels and gardens of the convent, Anna noticed a muffled shuffling behind her. Even as the sloshing water of the docks splashed in the rough tide, she could hear the footsteps gaining on her. Apparently Señor Scurvy didn't appreciate being made a fool of by a woman in the middle of a tavern surrounded by his shipmates.

She took the corner to her left at a good clip, spun 'round and bashed the man following her square on the shoulder, forcing him against the adobe building. "No me toques!" she shouted, holding her carved stick against him with all her weight.

The man shouted back something she didn't understand.

"Qué quieres?" she shouted and forced the end of the walking stick deeper into his shoulder. It was a good thing the man was tall, Anna caught herself thinking, or she might have taken his head off, or at least broken his nose. He was tall, much taller than Señor Scurvy, and though the light was low from a lantern on the nearby dock, the man's light-colored hair glowed. "Qué quieres?" she repeated.

"To pay your passage to England, if you'll let me."

~~~~~

Anna paused. Sebastian was staring wide eyed back at her. When he realized he wasn't moving, he cleared his throat and turned back to the river, nodding vaguely. She watched him for a moment, sure of his question.

"You can ask," she said.

He mumbled something then coughed again. "Um, no, go on with your story. This man wanted to give you money?"

She shook her head. "He did not ask for any *services,* if that's what you're worried about. The courtesans I spoke of were not me."

Sebastian turned red. "I didn't think that, I mean, that's not the kind of thing…"

She was amused by him—innocent but also not. Clever, but not about life. She reached out a hand to pat his shoulder. "You are a nice man, Sebastian."
~~~~~

This time he smiled back. "I'm glad you think so, Anna."

Sebastian turned to toss a pebble into the river as she told the rest of her story. The man was some kind of pilgrim on a journey of penance, who asked only to pay her passage and also to paint her portrait. She never saw his face, as he said it was part of his punishment.

Sebastian leaned in and watched her animated telling. How could she have brushed off an encounter like that? He'd have suspected the man was a robber or worse, but not Anna. She knew. This girl who'd been shipwrecked and saved by nuns, who played the fiddle with ease. Her with hair like hazel fire.

"His painting was wonderful, I thought, very skilled—like yours almost," Anna said. "But he seemed unhappy with it for some reason. I have found that artists tend to think poorly of their own work, why is that?"

Sebastian shrugged. He thought of his painting up in the third floor guest room where only the mice were enjoying it. The warmth of the stone underneath them was beginning to fade as the sun was setting.

"Um, if you'd like I can show you some of my other work…" he trailed off. Anna sat up straighter on the stone, the sun shone through her curls.

"Please do!"

Rumors or not, the next day as the sun began to rise,

Sebastian went to his workshop and Anna joined him. He handed her a cup of strong coffee and he led her to one end of the shop.

The room was narrow, but bright. A long row of windows cut through the long back wall, filling the room with sunlight. Dust motes drifted in the rays. Stacks of canvasses, some finished and others only with outlines, were piled against the walls of the small workshop. His easel stood facing the windows to gain the light. On a stand were brushes and a painter's palette. Anna picked up one brush and turned it over in her hand. Sebastian watched over his coffee mug. She ran her fingers over the carvings, the intricate vines.

"Much like the carvings the Sisters made, yet a different style, I believe." She considered the work like an artisan then continued to move about the workshop. She knew her way about the shop, as if she'd visited it many times.

Paint cans and brushes sat in a far corner on top of rough tarps. A small desk and stool were covered with papers and charcoal sketches. Anna leaned over to leaf through them.

"This one is of the Three Oaks bonfire." She glanced up at him. "Is this a fiddler?"

Unable to control the color of his face the way he could his paints, his cheeks flared red. He instead just nodded and sipped his coffee. Anna chuckled but pressed on.

"This fiddler seems to be a woman. Unless the stable hand now wears skirts?"

"Let's look at this one over here." He directed her to a canvas near the door with the beginnings of a painting of the willow tree and river.

The door slammed open and James rushed in. "Sebastian! You will not believe the things they are saying about you and the gypsy girl!" He had two mugs of coffee ready with one handed out to Sebastian when he realized he already had a cup. He turned to put the mug down on the worktable and saw Anna smiling at him. James paused, and she raised her mug to him then drank.

"What do you want to say, man?" Sebastian practically growled.

James hesitated.

"Um, they're saying you're, um, distracting her from her duties..." Sebastian glared at him. "But since you're Master Albright, I guess she works for you, or your father I mean, so it's up to you, sir, what the employees do for you—I mean how they help you with your needs—ah, I mean your, um art—" James fumbled about.

"James?"

"Yes, sir?"

"Get out."

James looked again at Anna who shook her head but smiled, then he made one of his false bows to Sebastian and winked. "Yes, sir!"

When the sound of James' jogging footsteps was gone, Anna burst out laughing and Sebastian joined her.

"Why do you and your valet both assume my ways are like those unfortunate ladies of the night?" she asked through her laughter.

But Sebastian stopped short. He looked at her again, the sunlight on her hair, the yellow patched skirt swishing as she held her stomach from her laughs. Her laughter slowed and then stopped when she saw the look on the young artist's face. He looked worried, and ashamed.

"Sebastian. Please, I only jest," she said with a serious face now. "I know the difference between men who are being gentlemen and those who look at a woman with, shall we say, motivations." She kept a lighthearted tone to her voice, but Sebastian could hear the tinge of knowing underneath.

He took a step closer to her. "I'm still sorry. I would never think such a thing about you." She saw the way his eyes pleaded that she not think poorly of him, and how he was hoping.

She set her mug on a table and walked up to him. She put her hand on his cheek and looked him in the eyes, seeing the blue and flecks of grey like the waves. She pulled him to her and kissed him. His arms wrapped around her waist in a way that felt exciting and safe. He felt the softness of her lips. She could smell linseed and coffee and grass. He felt her warmth and her hand in his hair. They held each other as the sun lit up the workshop.

Chapter 6

Three times James tried to apologize to Anna. Each time there was someone around and he would run out of the room. This time Anna was in the larder, helping Sylvia clean a salmon for the Albright's dinner later that night and he mumbled something about a "goat in the fields" when she stopped him.

"James," she said clearly. "You are quite a funny man, no wonder Sebastian calls you his friend." James opened his mouth but then only smiled and left.

"What was that for?" Sylvia asked as she chopped off a fin.

"Nothing." she laughed back.

A clamor of footsteps sounded from the main kitchen with echoes of "ma'am" and "Mrs. Albright." Caroline swept into the larder wearing her usual shade of green with a light pink shawl around her shoulders. Anna and Sylvia bobbed curtsies and waited for her to speak.

"Girls, is this the main dinner?" she asked, wrinkling her nose at the fish.

"Yes, ma'am, the salmon is fresh from the river," Sylvia piped up.

"Hmm." Caroline's response wasn't clear. She rounded the table and Anna could feel her eyes on her.

"How have the sheep been grazing?" Caroline directed her

question to Anna.

"Well, Mrs. Albright."

"That's not much of an answer, is it? I need details. To know if their wool will be ready for adding to my clothing. Customers only want the best." She looked Anna over, seeing the patches on her skirt. "That may not be important for gypsies, but respectable people take pride in their appearance."

"I am not a gypsy, ma'am." Anna spoke in an accent that though different was not the way the other servants spoke. Her tone and diction were as if she had been at least schooled, if not educated thoroughly. Caroline froze.

"Let me apologize, dear," she said. Anna waited. Sylvia swallowed hard.

"What kind of plants have the sheep been eating?" Caroline moved on, looking at the shelves on the walls as if they held important things and not extra spices.

"The sheep mostly eat grasses, clovers, and other flowers," Anna explained.

"Like royal thyme?" Caroline said, her back to the other women. Anna and Sylvia exchanged glances.

"Yes, those too. Though I've been told you call them violets."

Caroline twirled around and looked at Anna. She batted her eyes a few times and her lips curled into a small smirk in the corner.

"Make sure to keep a good eye on the sheep when you're out grazing them. Wouldn't want any distractions," Caroline said offhand as she turned towards the larder door. "Throw out that fish and get another, Sylvia. I don't care for its look."

Sylvia let out a great sigh once Caroline was gone, and tossed the fish on the garbage heap. "At least you get to enjoy the fields again," she said to Anna as she hobbled back to the table.

"Yes, I will," Anna said.

Sebastian met her out in the grazing fields the next day, like so many other days over the last month. He brought his easel and paints sometimes, other times just a sketchbook. Today was his book and a set of pencils. He sat under a scrub oak while she walked off with the sheep. His pencil captured her on the hillside, the breeze blowing her hair. At lunch she joined him there to see the sketches and rested on a rough blanket until he became tired of sketching and they reached for each other instead.

The rumors began to spread, again.

One morning as Sylvia was picking up the Albright's bakery order, a man asked her if she had healed from the curse of the gypsy girl. She told him to shove himself in the backside and stomped out. When she sat for a moment near the fountain in the square she overheard a group of women claiming that the young Master Albright had been put under a spell and that Caroline Albright was worried for her stepson's future.

Anna didn't care, she told Sylvia that afternoon as they hung linens out to dry. "Let them talk, it means nothing to us."

"Us?" Sylvia prodded her. Anna flicked out a damp sheet and flung it over a line. Sylvia reached for the next sheet and a handful of clothespins. To her, Anna was beginning to look different than the girl who asked why servants wore hats and not braids. She looked like a person who knew things.

"Where were you going when you were shipwrecked?" Sylvia asked. Anna stood with a pillow sham in her hands midway to the line, her jaw dropped a bit and she let out a breath. Sylvia continued, "You told Mrs. Albright you aren't a gypsy, and you told me you hadn't heard of England before. I thought maybe you were an American, since you talk so strange, and I've never really met one before. But now I'm wondering, where were you going?"

Anna shuttered a bit. Her hands trembled and the sheets shook.

"You scared to tell me? 'Cus I won't say anything to the Albrights or nobody. I'm not like the other maids, you know?"

"I know that," Anna whispered. She moved to a footstool and sat. She held a basket of clean linen on her lap. "I am sorry, you have been so kind…" Anna looked past the clotheslines to the hillside. "I was searching for my grandfather. He's…missing."

"And you thought he'd be in Spain?" Sylvia offered. There was more here, she knew.

"No, but I looked there. And here in England." She shuttered, her voice shaking. "There was this man, a lying, scheming, evil son of a bitch—" She glanced up when Sylvia gasped at her curse. "It is the truth. But this man, he did…something. I know it. And my Grandad…he's just gone." Her hands clutched a sheet so tight that water wrung out and dripped down her knuckles. "And now I'm here. There's nothing more to be said."

"My lord!" Sylvia muttered. "And the man?"

"Don't ask me about him, Sylvia. He's evil, and I'll speak not about him again."

"Do you plan to keep looking for your grandpa?" she asked.

Anna stood back up and started laying the sheet on the line. "I'm not even sure where to look if I do."

For a few minutes they were silent. The final sheet had been put up and small bouquets of lavender sprigs were pinned between the sheets to freshen them. They began gathering their baskets when Sylvia stopped. Anna turned and looked at her friend. "Is there something else, Sylvia?" She glanced around for a missed linen or basket.

"You're in love."

Anna let out a chuckle of agreement and a broad smile filled her face, worry forgotten. "You could say that."

"And Master Albright?" Sylvia asked.

Anna shrugged but pulled out the sketch Sebastian had done

of her playing fiddle at Three Oaks.

"He also made me a beautiful painting of the river. It is on a canvas he rolled up in a leather case."

Sylvia nodded.

Then Anna went back to her pocket for a small pouch and fished out a wooden coin from among the few real ones she had earned. She had carved a picture of the willow tree on one side of the coin, and a paintbrush on the other. "I'm fairly certain he'll like this," she sighed.

"That's bad," Sylvia muttered.

"Really?" Anna turned her wooden coin over again.

"No, I mean that carving is lovely. But this"—she gestured to the coin and sketch—"is bad. He's Master Albright, not a servant or a stable hand. And you, um, are a—wanderer," Sylvia trailed off, surprised that she could think of a word other than gypsy.

"So?" Anna looked startled and also perplexed, not understanding why her friend seemed worried.

"Never mind." Sylvia hadn't the heart to tell her how things worked, when she obviously had no idea, and seemed so happy.

~~~~~

A few days later, the Sow's Ear tavern sat quiet. The tavern owner's wife stood muttering something about the high price of potatoes. Her husband went on ignoring her, filling the mugs of the
~~~~~

few patrons and wiping down the polished oak bar.

On the wall a wanted poster was pinned among the "pigs for sale" and "hands for hire" ads. A familiar face with wild red hair sneered out from under a top hat on a "wanted for questions" poster.

The door swung open letting the breeze tumble in from the cobblestone street.

"Ah, Sebastian, close the bleedin' door, will ya?" The tavern owner chided, dropping his towel on the bar and pulling his overcoat tight against his neck.

"Eh, Mac, you're too sensitive!" Sebastian pulled up a stool at the bar, laughing at the tavern owner.

"Ha, this coming from a painter." Mac filled a mug with ale and slid it over to Sebastian. The ale sloshed over and onto the bar.

"Every time!" His wife scolded, sending the tavern patrons into a fit of laughter.

"So, tell me, Sebastian"—Mac wiped up the ale—"what's this talk of you and a gypsy girl?"

Sebastian sipped his ale and examined the countertop. "Not sure what you mean, Mac."

"Ah, well that means it's true." Mac snickered.

"I heard'ed she's a witch," a fat man sitting down the bar slurred over his mug. It was hard to believe that someone so awkward could manage to balance on the barstool.

"Aye, I heard same." Mac agreed. "A boy from yer father's

place was in just this week and said she was workin' magic on another girl's foot."

"You shouldn't listen to gossip." Sebastian turned around. "That goes for you too, friend." The fat man hiccupped and guzzled more of his drink.

"Sebastian, is it true you've been carousing with a gypsy girl?" Mac's wife wandered up and embraced him about the shoulders. "'Cus, you know, witch or no, gypsies are not to be trusted."

"Her name is Anna, and there was no carousing, Martha."

"Ah, well you know I worry 'bout ya, Sebastian." She smiled. "Someone's got to look out for ya, boy." Sebastian shook his head and went back to his drink. Martha took the signal and returned to her figures.

"Pay her no heed, Sebastian. It's good a young man get his fun while he can. It ends awful quick," Mac added under his breath. Martha slapped her husband across the shoulder.

"Woman!" Mac yelped and rubbed the spot she hit. Of course this sent the few patrons into laughter again.

"Tell me, dear." Martha turned to Sebastian, ignoring her grumbling husband and the laughing drunks. "Where is the gypsy—I mean Anna—from?"

Sebastian paused with his glass to his lips. He thought for a moment about the wooden coin in his pocket. Anna had given it to him the other day as they sat in the field. On one side was a carved relief of a tree, a willow—their willow. The other side had a paintbrush and a setting sun. *Sister Maria taught me a bit of their carving.* Anna had blushed when he'd kissed her cheek in thanks.

"Well, she came here from Spain."

"Spain?"

"Yeah, Martha, Spain."

"Funny, she doesn't look like a Spaniard."

Sebastian shook his head again. "I didn't say she's a Spaniard. She was there, now she's here."

Martha nodded. "Ah, so she's English." Sebastian clutched his drink a bit tighter.

"Ah, woman, let the boy be," Mac said. She shrugged and walked to the other end of the bar to gather up empty ale mugs.

"Well, she's a pretty lass. I'm sure that Caroline is ever so happy her stepson is carousing with a gypsy."

"Martha!"

"For the love of Pete! I wasn't carousin' with anyone," Sebastian shouted, his eyes wide and his cheeks growing red.

"Leave the boy be, woman." Mac threw his towel at Martha and missed. The lopsided drunk fell from his stool laughing.

The whole of the Sow's Ear watched while the large drunk shook himself off and attempted to regain his perch on the bar stool. Like an awkward robin swallowing a wriggling worm, the man straightened his red vest, gripped the mug, and downed the last of the ale.

"So tell me, Sebastian"—Mac slid another ale to the drunken robin— "what was all the rowdy stuff with your pop? Heard ya told him where he could go?"

"Like I said before, Mac, you shouldn't listen to gossip."

"Aye, you're right. I sound like a woman." Martha walked by with a tray of dirty mugs and smacked her husband on the back of his head. Sebastian almost dropped his ale laughing this time, all talk of gypsy girls forgotten.

"Woman! Yer makin' me look bad."

"Don't need my help," she called back as she turned the corner into the kitchen.

Mac grumbled under his breath but turned back to the young painter. "So was it all true?"

Sebastian sat looking at the mug, shifting it around in a slow circle. "Partly."

"I knew it! Good on ya. Here," Mac darted away and returned a moment later with another mug. "On the house, Sebastian."

"Damn it, Mac."

"No, you take it—for doing what I've always wanted to." Mac was grinning like a proverbial cat with a fish in its jaws. So Sebastian had no choice but to finish off the first mug, then take a long gulp out of the second as Mac watched.

"Thanks."

"A'course." Mac went back to polishing the bar.

"Never knew you hated my father so much." The grin fell off Mac's face as quickly as it had appeared.

"Ah, well…"

"No worries…my father is a pompous ass." Sebastian finished off the second mug.

"Well, now, he's not all bad." Mac's words stretched out. Sebastian raised an eyebrow.

"Oh really?"

"Why just the other day he was going on and on about you to that fancy-dressed guy."

Sebastian stopped mid-gulp and coughed a bit. "What fancy-dressed guy?"

"Not sure really. He was wearing a nice waistcoat and carried a pearl-topped cane. Him an yer pop sat at the table by the fire. I remember 'cus the fancy-dressed man blocked the heat." Mac shivered slightly.

"Well, what did they talk about?"

"Oh, Sebastian, you know I don't listen to other folks' conversations."

"Ha!" His wife laughed from the kitchen.

"Well, maybe I heard a bit of it." Mac scowled in the direction of the kitchen.

"Mind letting me know?" Sebastian asked again.

Mac poured himself an ale and downed half at once. "He sold yer painting to that man."

"What?" Sebastian stumbled off the barstool, spilling the rest of his ale. The drunken robin-man burst out laughing and almost tipped from the stool again.

"What?" Sebastian yelled again. The few other patrons of the Sow's Ear stopped talking and watched him. "He did what?"

"Keep it down," Mac whispered. His wife poked her head around the kitchen corner.

"I can't believe it." Sebastian sat down again.

"Well, I heard him say something about you being so talented. That your stuff seems so real." Mac tried to calm Sebastian down, who was beginning to tremble, and pushed another ale in front of him.

"The hell with him!" Sebastian roared again. "He thinks he can do this?" He slammed back the pint, dragged his sleeve across his mouth and pounded the empty mug on the bar. "Thanks for the ale, Mac." Sebastian tossed a couple coins on the bar.

"Where you going?"

Sebastian flung open the door, letting in the cold night breeze.

~~~~~
~~~~~

The fireplace in the Albright parlor filled the room with yellow light. The flames cast a flickering pattern on the Oriental rug on the polished wood floor. In the corner, Mrs. Albright's green cloak hung on a brass coat rack, golden embroidered stars twinkling in the firelight.

Warmth and tea was all Mr. Albright was looking forward to that night. Mrs. Albright was chattering on about the latest gossip in town and how Lady Chadwick was coming next week from Dover to have a dress made, and that Lord Chadwick was said to have just made quite a bit from his investment in a rather well producing tin mine.

"Interesting, dear," Mr. Albright said over his edition of the evening news.

"We must have them to dinner while they are here, dear," Caroline suggested.

"Of course."

"I'll arrange it then." Caroline poured herself more tea from a pot with pale pink roses. The sleeves of her jade silk dress were like vines to the pink rose teacup. Just as she set the teapot back on its silver tray, the door to the parlor slammed open.

"Father!" Sebastian shouted. Mr. and Mrs. Albright jumped to their feet in such surprise. Clara, the maid, was in the hall with a tray of biscuits but turned quickly out of sight, but most likely not out of earshot.

"Sebastian? What is the matter, son? You quite scared your stepmother and I."

"Well, my apologies then, *stepmother*." Sebastian feigned a deep bow, his arms stretched out wide to the sides.

"Accepted, dear," Caroline said, and resumed her seat.

"Well, now that that is out of the way, where the hell do you two get the right to sell *my* paintings!" Sebastian yelled again. Caroline looked shocked. "That was a birthday gift for you, *stepmother*. It is bad enough you moved it to that dust-filled repository on the third floor, but now you sell it?"

"Oh, Sebastian, it isn't that I did not appreciate your gift—"

"Obviously!"

"But, it just wasn't my…style, dear."

Sebastian nodded and rubbed his face. "You mean like that cloak, right?" He pointed and Caroline turned to gaze at it.

"Well, yes, actually. I mean this once was owned by a princess of Algiers—"

"The hell it was! That man was a swindler!" Sebastian yelled. "And you, Father, were taken in like a common fool."

"Now just a minute, I know a good deal when I see one." Mr. Albright drew himself up tall and smoothed his combover.

"Sure you do, Father." Sebastian shot a glance at Caroline and she furrowed her brow in confusion. Sebastian sat down in a chair next to the fireplace, and put his head in his hands. His pants were covered in dry paint and grease again, and Caroline flinched as she reached out and touched his knee.

"Sebastian, have you been drinking?"

He grimaced.

"I know you are upset at your father," Caroline went on, "but understand that he is just looking out for you. You tend to make bad decisions, dear."

Sebastian mumbled something, but Caroline continued. "You are a businessman's son who paints and goes to taverns." Sebastian glanced at his father who quickly took to examining the clock on the mantle. "And you go around with gypsy girls." Caroline patted his knee.

Sebastian jumped up and paced the parlor floor.

From his workshop that morning he had watched as Anna led the sheep over the western hill to pasture. He had stood by the window and imagined her walking down past the weeping willow and drinking from the stream. She would be carrying her walking stick with the special symbols the Spanish nuns had made for her. Anna would lean down and pick a violet for her hair, the flower she called royal thyme. And she'd gaze to the west like she did sometimes, like she was lost in a dream or searching the horizon for someone.

Or at least he thought it had been Anna.

"What did you do?" Sebastian turned to his father. Mr.

Albright coughed and tugged at his waist coat.

"We couldn't have our son going about with a gypsy." Caroline's nose raised a bit higher and she took a sip of tea. "I heard she was doing curses."

"She was helping to heal that other girl's ankle! She learned it from nuns, for God's sake."

Caroline shrugged and placed her teacup on the table. "And how do you know that, Sebastian?"

Mr. Albright nodded and crossed his arms. "Well?"

Sebastian pounded his fist on the mantle. "She told me so."

"Ah." Caroline fluttered her eyelashes just slightly. "Well, no matter, she was dismissed this morning."

Sebastian lunged towards Caroline, but stopped in the middle of the room. "What?"

"It is better that way, Sebastian." Mr. Albright lit his pipe.

"Is that so?"

"Why yes," Caroline said. "You should be concentrating on your art."

Sebastian's head spun and he now regretted that fourth ale, or was it fifth?

"My art?"

"Yes, Sebastian," Caroline explained. "While I didn't care for it, some people do. As artists, we need to understand what the buyer wants."

Sebastian leaned against the mantelpiece. "I'll not let you sell my paintings, Father."

"But think of how famous you could be, Sebastian," Mr. Albright said.

"You mean how much money I'd make—for you, Father?"

"Sebastian," Caroline scolded.

"Like you're any better, Caroline!" Sebastian swung around and stared into the shocked face of his stepmother. "Don't pretend you kept that dress shop as a hobby. I know damn well it's to get more coins for you and Father. And you are no artist, Caroline." Sebastian pointed in her face. "I know your poor assistant, Lucy, does all the work. You just parade around like a high-class…courtesan, fluttering in those silken dresses. One more coin from a lady, one more business deal from a lord."

"That is enough, Sebastian!" Mr. Albright yelled as he moved to Caroline's side and put an arm around the whimpering dress maker. "Look, you've made your mother cry."

It was like Sebastian's stomach was slammed against his spine. His fists shook and a drop of blood ran between his fingers.

"Sebastian!" Mr. Albright yelled from the doorway of the parlor, but his son was already bounding down the second floor hallway to his rooms.

James stood in his doorway, a bag in each hand.

"It's time, isn't it, sir?"

"You're damn right, James."

<div align="center">~~~~~</div>

Sebastian stood atop the large boulder. The water was running high from all the runoff, and the rushes shuffled in the breeze. His hair blew back from his face and he squinted into the wind. James sat below on the shore, their bags next to him. In the cave Sebastian's box of paints laid open, supplies strewn about.

His hands were caked with shades of bright yellow paint. They were shaking.

Sebastian looked down at the carved paintbrush in his right hand that his father had bought from that snake oil salesman Goodfellow. It was also covered in yellow—he didn't bother cleaning it. Looking up, Sebastian raised his arm over his head and flung the caked brush into the stream.

Chapter 7

Sebastian and James arrived at the Republic Alehouse only to find the windows shuttered and wooden planks nailed across the door. James peaked through a knothole in the shutters.

"Chairs are all upturned, like they haven't been touched since that brawl on Saturday."

"Wonder if C.R. skipped town."

"No idea. You'd think the gents would've heard something," James replied.

"It's too bad." Sebastian shaded his eyes to see inside the abandoned alehouse. "C.R. made one hell of a house ale. Reminded me of Mac's."

James nodded. "Well"—he clapped his hands together—"where to now, sir?" Sebastian punched his friend's shoulder. "Ah, sorry, old habits and all that." James laughed.

"I'm guessing the lads have an alternative place. Shall we go find them?"

"After you, sir." James bowed and Sebastian gave him a good push.

Life in Port City was making a transition—the speed and drama of the day was taking a deep breath, kicking off its shoes, and relaxing for the evening. Closed signs were being hung in the shop windows, and keys were turning in their locks. Wrought iron gates guarded doorways. A jeweler gathered the sparkling wares from his front window to stash them away for the night in a place where thugs and roustabouts wouldn't find them.

But not everyone was ready to pack up and sleep away the dark hours. Like a night shift at a dock, a wave of folks moved into the streets. In the yellow light of smudged street lanterns, shadows slipped across the stone walls of the buildings. Those stones were the only things still reminiscent of the blazing summer sun. They radiated heat, and for the poor soul who bumped an uncovered arm against them, a reflex was bound to trigger snapping the arm back— and perhaps a colorful word or two.

Many of the shadows moved in the same direction, towards the sound of lively music. The port city's pied pipers drew the people to alehouses or into small squares, some which were hardly large enough to be an intersection in the day.

As James and Sebastian strolled the darkened city streets, they too followed the sounds of music and laughter that echoed off the tall stone buildings. One street they turned down was so narrow, Sebastian fell a step behind so he and James wouldn't touch shoulders, or worse still, the stone walls. From above wind chimes hung out a window tinkled in the slightest breeze. The salty air swept in from the marina, which was only a few streets to the west, and once they heard the waves splashing against the pier mix with the echoing music, Sebastian swung around the next corner.

Walking past the fishmonger's stall, now empty for the night but with a stink that lingered far past market time, the men came upon a group of musicians playing a lively dance tune. One man was tapping out the beat on a small drum while another played a tune on a flute. A girl of about nine spun around shaking a tambourine in time with the beat. Her blond curls were tied up in a yellow kerchief, and her dress was patched with swatches of green wool.

People were scattered about the small square eating and drinking ale poured from a barrel. Some sat along the edge of a bubbling fountain, the brass figure of a boar lounging in the center of the water. Other folks were propped up on old crates, dragged there from the docks most likely. A group of men sat playing at cards. The stranger sight was the woman who had joined the game. The pile of copper in front of her was much larger than that of the men, though they didn't seem to mind.

The square may have been small, but the buildings that made it were taller than any Sebastian had seen in his former life. The height and small area added an ethereal tone to the music's lively tempo. Although there was no bonfire, Sebastian was reminded of all the nights spent at Three Oaks with James and the other servants of his father's house. Ever since arriving in Port City almost six months earlier they'd spent their evenings in places like C.R.'s tavern or small squares such as this one, and their days moving cargo on the docks.

"Mate, what happened to the alehouse?" James shook the hand of a short, stocky man standing next to a beer barrel with RA branded on the top. Sebastian saw James wince a bit when he shook the man's hand—could have torn James' arm out of his socket, had Kellogg wanted. The burly gent had a foot up on a crate making him seem slightly taller than he was. But though he only came a bit short of James' average height, Kellogg had a box-like shape that came from many years of loading and unloading merchant ships.

"Ah, the hell with C.R. If he didn't have the wit not to get in with money-mongers, then good riddance."

"Did he really?" James' eyes were as wide as Kellogg's grin.

"I ain't sayin' a thing. Here mate, have an ale." Kellogg waved a woman over who was carrying wooden mugs on a tray. James recognized her as one of the former barmaids from CR's. Sebastian was delighted with the way people in Port City could find ways to indulge even when the local tavern owner had gone "missing."

"And one for you, Sketch?"

"Any doubt?" Like so many people who leave their former lives behind, Sebastian had not only renounced his surname, but had been dubbed Sketch by his fellow dockworkers when they saw him drawing on a discarded plank with a charred bit of wood. The new name stuck.

Kellogg passed Sebastian a mug, then turned to take a mug

for himself and let out a sharp whistle. James choked a little on his drink. The blond girl with the tambourine froze and stared back at Kellogg who was shaking his head. The girl frowned, her shoulders drooping, and put down the ale mug she'd pinched from an unobservant reveler.

"She thinks 'cus she's pretty no one'll suspect her."

James laughed and clapped Kellogg's back. "Now, why should that worry you, papa?"

"Aye, it'll be my constant worry in a few years, I reckon," Kellogg said, watching his daughter return to dancing with the musicians.

"So, is this the plan now? Drinking ale and dancing in the streets?" Sebastian asked.

Kellogg shrugged. "If needs be, Sketch. It's a fair bit better than sitting at home thinking of all the crates that'll be arriving on the *Horse Dawn* tomorrow."

"I'll drink to that." James agreed.

Sebastian tossed up a hand. "All right—to drinking in the street." The men charged their mugs and downed the last bit of C.R.'s ale.

The crowd cheered as the dance tune ended and another began. This time though the flute player had turned his attention to an ale-maid, and a fiddler stepped up. He propped a foot up on a wooden crate and called out "For the lovers!" Cheers again greeted the new dance song. Though not as quick a tune as the last, most people whose mugs were empty took to twirling their ladies around the square. A few passersby stopped to clap for an elderly gent who gently turned his smiling wife a few times and pecked her rosy cheek. The couple drifted on into the flowing tributaries of the city.

"That fiddler ain't too bad, huh boys?" Kellogg asked. "Got quite a nice rhythm."

"Hey!" James wasn't listening to Kellogg. He was watching Sebastian's darkening form slip away down a nearby alley.

"Where'd he go off to?"

James let out a long breath. "I could use another ale, Kellogg."

Nothing in Port City was immune to the salt. It would get in between the cobblestones, wearing them thin. So when Sebastian turned the corner of the alleyway and tripped on the loose cobble he wasn't truly surprised. James had tripped not three days earlier near the docks of all places, in plain sight of the men. Many were still calling James "Gimp" because the fun of it hadn't worn off.

But as Sebastian was rising up from the warm street, the thing that surprised him most was how little he hurt. Guess he figured falling with your knee onto hard stone would cause some kind of pain.

He shook his boot out to his side like a dog and carried on down the alley. At the next corner he realized he was still holding the wooden ale cup so he tossed it aside. The crash of hollow wood on cobbles echoed up the tall buildings and many people on the cross street turned to see what had made such a racket.

For Sebastian, all he heard was the fiddle. Turning his eyes away from the onlookers, he set off down the street at a steady march. Street lantern after street lantern cast yellow light on him, and he tried to listen to the scuffle of his own feet on the salted stones. At the next road, people were milling around a large fountain. He'd reached the city center and joined the strands of people circling the fountain like the current swirling around a stone in a stream.

Even with the ale party blocks behind him, a part of Sebastian could still hear that damn fiddle, the bow stringing out a lively tune made for couples to kick up their heels.

He spun around and bumped into a lean man with fiery red hair. The man was linked arm-in-arm with a young girl with short blond locks. "Hey, careful there," the man said and his lady giggled. It was actually more of a cackle, one better used by witches than a young girl on a nighttime stroll with her suitor.

"My apologies, ma'am, sir," Sebastian mumbled while shooting past them.

Again he turned up the closest street. This one had no doors and no windows on any of the lower levels, and no light spilled from any street lanterns. He quickened his pace and at the end of the alley he paused to take a deep breath—he hadn't realized he'd be holding it. Ahead was the front of a small church. No lights were lit so late in the evening, which was no surprise to him really. He wondered if the friars who ran this little parish would be anything like the sisters of Colina Roja. Perhaps they too knew the art of wood carving.

He put one hand in his pocket and pulled out the small wooden coin. He looked on the carved relief of the willow, and flipped it to see the sunset and paintbrush. When they unpacked their bags at Mrs. Holding's boarding house, Sebastian pulled it from the bottom of his bag.

"What's that?" James had asked. Sebastian had turned it over and saw the willow tree.

"A good-bye."

But of course these friars wouldn't be interested in such crafts. No, the residents of Port City knew the friars had the best luck at fishing. No beggar was ever turned away from their door, as long as they liked whiting.

Sebastian looked up from the willow-wood coin. None of the closed-up shops looked familiar. He realized he'd been walking and paused under a street lantern, now growing dull, to see if he could get his bearings. The city center fountain should be to the north of the dock, but where was the dock? He cocked his head to the side, thinking he'd listen for the waves, but put a hand out to the lantern post to steady himself. The dizziness was stronger than a normal extra-round of ale caused him and he shook his head a bit.

"Looks like someone's had one too many, eh lads?" A throaty voice chuckled from behind. A couple more jeers and laughs rose up to join in. "What say you let us give ya a hand?"

Sebastian turned around as slow as he could without seeming particularly drunk. It was hard to tell how many laughing boys there were since they stood just outside the ring of light from the dull lantern.

"I'm good, friends. Just needed a moment." He raised his hand to his head in a semi-salute. The golden brown of the polished willow-wood coin gleamed in the yellow lamp light and the first shadow darted up and grabbed Sebastian's hand.

The dizziness vanished. Sebastian's mind cleared of its fog and he snapped his hand back. The shadow whistled and the others started towards him.

Sebastian swung his fist out to the right and connected with something soft just outside of the ring of light. As that person hit the cobble stones and let out a wail of "mama," another of the brutes came at him from the left. Sebastian hopped to the right and the brute missed, hitting the lamp poll instead. The rather heavy man leaned away, clutching his fist and moaning. Sebastian couldn't help but laugh at the sight of the two muggers: one clutching his hand and the other roiling on the ground calling for his mother. He continued to laugh as the third man, the one with the throaty chuckle, tapped his shoulder. Sebastian turned that direction and realized his mistake a second too late—like most mistakes—and ended up on the ground shaking his head again from the ringing.

"That'll teach ya," his attacker said. The lead brute loomed over Sebastian. His mustache was thick and he came so close Sebastian could see the bits and pieces of food caked in his bristles. The corners of the brute's mouth lifted and he let out his throaty chuckle again.

"Aye, that does teach me," Sebastian agreed. "Teaches me how to do this!" he swung out his left leg and swept it under the brute's legs. The lead brute took a very hard seat on the cobbles next to the mother-caller and the fist-holder.

Instead of waiting for the attacker's next move, Sebastian jumped up and ran. "Goodnight, gents!" he called back to them.

Chapter 8

Every table was full in the coffeehouse the next morning. Dock owners and merchants sat discussing politics and trade laws while travelers awaited their ships, destined for foreign lands. Sailors told fish tales and boasted of the dangers they'd encountered in their travels. Each one sipped their exotic roasted drink with no thought as to the strange places the beans had grown.

Sebastian sat savoring his drink. He hoped the hot brew would chase away his blinding headache. The roast was dark and bitter despite him cutting it with a bit of cream, even though the shop keeper had called him "miss" when he had asked for it. He was in no mood to reply in his usual mocking way, as was surely the hope of the shopkeeper.

He wanted to squint, to keep the light out, but then his left eye would blaze hot, forcing them open again. Once he found a spot that worked he focused all his energy on not moving his head.

Sebastian touched the underside of his left eye ever so slightly, not really sure what good it would do. The blood-filled pouch throbbed. It was hot and felt heavy on his face. He honestly couldn't remember if the brute last night had made contact with his eye—much of that whole scene was fuzzy. But he was pretty much unharmed and still had his coins, both metal and wooden.

A good smack to the head mixed with off-ale makes for a

dismal morning, he thought, and moving crates off a ship in the blazing sun just wasn't going to happen.

Sebastian chuckled—then stopped quickly and put a hand to his forehead.

"Argh," he moaned under his breath.

He sipped his coffee.

Among the traders and sailors in the coffeehouse, Sebastian caught the face of Winston the foreman, sitting near the back, his head over his cup. He quickly turned away hoping Winston didn't notice him, given that he was supposed to be off-loading cargo an hour ago. But he turned away too quickly, and his throbbing head spun.

Looking to his right, Sebastian noticed a man in a burgundy overcoat sitting near the fireplace. The grate was not lit, not in this heat. Light shone through a skylight and hit the man's silver hair just right that it almost glowed. A brown top hat sat on the man's table next to his coffee cup.

"Sketch!" Winston was standing on his left. He was a man of about sixty with grey hair and shoulders that pulled back from his chest as if he was always standing at attention.

"Morning, sir."

"Aren't you supposed to be unloading the *Horse Dawn* right now?"

"I was just leaving."

"That's what I thought!" Winston called after him.

Four carriages lined the docks, each pulled by two dappled ponies that snorted and stamped, obviously unhappy with being harnessed in the heat.

Sebastian rounded the corner at a quick, limping trot but stopped fast. He leaned up against the last carriage and gazed at the ship anchored at the dock. Even with sails tied the *Horse Dawn* dominated the port. This clipper was not to be bet against. For some reason, Sebastian was surprised at this. Most of the ships that anchored here shrunk once their sails and riggings were stowed, so that hulls and masts blended into an indistinguishable mass.

There was something familiar about this ship. For a brief moment the painting he made for his stepmother flashed in his mind—and the dark ship he added afterward. He rubbed his forehead and threw the thought out of his mind. He waved to James as he skirted the row of carriages and made his way up the loading ramp.

"Ah, your eye!" James' face contorted into a mix of shock, disgust, and curiosity. "What the hell happened?"

"I fell."

"Aye, onto the fist of Chance Porter and his brutes." Kellogg laughed and slapped Sebastian's back. He rocked forward and clutched his forehead, again. "Oh, dealin' with the ale there, Sketch?"

"You're damn right. Where'd you get that stuff, Kellogg?"

Kellogg winked. "Bit ya did it? No more than you did to Chance Porter, I hear."

"Gimp! Get back on it!" the foreman yelled. Sebastian wondered if Winston was still carrying his coffee cup.

James slunk off to the loading ramp to move another crate from the *Horse Dawn*.

"So, tell me Kellogg, who is this Porter guy I roughed up last night?"

Kellogg started walking to the ramp and Sebastian followed, limping as little as possible.

"Just your typical pickpocket type and his rabble." Kellogg stooped low and heaved a crate onto his shoulder. Sebastian scooted around to the other side as he turned down the ramp, out of view of the foreman. "Chance is the type to steal from a lone woman or a child. Doesn't usually go for a grown man."

"Well thanks."

"Unless he was flat out sloshed."

Sebastian thought about the night before. He remembered making for the other side of town when the fiddler started and there was a man with red hair and a blond woman who cackled like a witch, but after that much of it was a haze. Damn ale.

"Well I wouldn't have been sloshed if my friend hadn't given me questionable ale. And don't tell me it was C.R.'s."

"Oh beggars-n-choosers, mate," Kellogg scoffed and

dropped the crate in the back of a carriage. "But I'd keep yer eyes open. You made him quite the fool. Damn, wish I'd-a seen it!" He laughed.

"Well if you'd been there to see it, then he might not have given me this." Sebastian pointed to his eye.

Kellogg laughed again and shoved Sebastian towards the loading ramp.

The crates pulled out of the hold of the *Horse Dawn* were quite irregular. All other cargo Sebastian had seen thus far were bleached wooden crates, each of typical sizes and shapes, quite unremarkable save for the name of an owner or place of delivery. The men now were moving a miss-matched variety of long, skinny boxes, small rectangular parcels tied into groups of four, and one large crate that required three men to move.

Stranger still, each container was painted colors. One had a side painted red and another box's top was yellow. One of the parcels-of-four was varying shades of red, like the sky at sunset. The larger crate was blue on one side and green on another.

"You ever seen cargo like this?" James asked Kellogg.

"Can't say I have. Looks like the crates are ready for St. Chris' day!"

Sebastian surveyed the crates piling up on the dock. The colors were so vibrant in the hot mid-morning sun that he wondered how on earth they stayed like that in the hold of a clipper ship. With the humidity and water, no stain would remain so bright. "Could the colors be a marking for something?" he asked.

"For what?"

"Not sure—maybe we're to send them somewhere different? Or sort them, you know, green with green, red with red?"

Kellogg shook his head. "Not unless we're to split this 'un here in two." He pointed at a long, skinny box that was yellow on one side and red on the other.

Sebastian stooped over and picked up a box with a green top. The pigment wiped onto his hands. "Ah, blazes!"

The other dock workers laughed. "Painting yer'self for Chris' day, Sketch?" a tall worker with a bald head sniggered while he walked by with a blue box on his shoulder.

"Think the sun'll roast the shine off your marble, Dover?" Sebastian called after him.

"That's funny. None rubbed off that red one I moved." Kellogg hitched his thumb back at the line of carriages and horses— now very impatient and telling them so.

"Not that blue one either," James added, tossing Sebastian a bit of canvas tarp that was lying nearby.

"Guess it just adds to my perfect morning," Sebastian said, wiping his hands as the foreman was heading towards them.

Being docked a half a day's pay for showing up late, Sebastian threw up his hands, still tinted green from the cargo box, dropped a few words gentlemen only say when women aren't around, and left. James was not at all impressed by his former boss' attitude, especially when he came back to their room at the boarding house and found him passed out on his bed—one hand clutching a bottle, the other the wooden coin.

James dropped his work boot on the floor near Sebastian's head.

"Ah dammit, James!"

"Oh, I'm sorry, *sir*. Did my boot dropping wake you?" He leaned over and took the bottle from him. "Glad to know we had enough money to buy brandy." He chucked the bottle onto the table.

Sebastian sat up but hung his head. "For the love of God, James."

James didn't say anything more, but threw him a damp cloth. He wiped his forehead, then attempted to clean off more of the green pigment.

James stomped about their room, changed out of his dirty work clothes, and opened the curtains. Sebastian squinted in the bright light, much like the morning, he realized. James slammed a cup of water into his hand.

"They dock you half a day's pay and you call the foreman a 'damn fool who wouldn't know his ass from the head of a donkey.' What in the blazes were you thinking?"

"It's true: that man is a fool."

"He was going to fire you but Kellogg saved you."

"Remind me to punch him." James scowled. "Just a joke, mate. I'll thank him tomorrow."

James opened the window and a salty breeze moved the curtains.

"Oh, buck up, James." Sebastian got up and joined his friend at the window. Squinting out towards the pier, he could see the top mast of the *Horse Dawn* above the rooftops.

"Besides, my mother always said faces like that tend to stick that way." James snorted. "Ah, don't worry, we'll make do." Sebastian tilted back the cup of water.

"Not the point. I know we'll make do." James turned away from the window. Sebastian watched his eyes hesitate on a black sack in the corner.

"No worries. Now, tell me about that barmaid from last night."

James' ears turned red, but he proceeded to tell his friend about the lovely girl who was ever so impressed that James once met the Lord of Oakbrook.

"The Lord of *Where?*" Sebastian raised an eyebrow, and James let out a wild snicker, bottle of brandy now forgotten.

James slipped out early the next morning, so Sebastian decided to refresh their limited supplies. Mrs. Holding would only rent to dock workers if they contributed to the pantry.

The market at the docks was full after the many ships arrived the day before. Stands were bursting with vegetables and fruits, some he didn't recognize. One stall held brightly colored lanterns and rugs weaved in far off India. Spices filled the air with the scents of cardamom and allspice. A flower merchant had live geraniums from Rome—most were the brightest of reds, but there were some of a delicate pink. Another booth was packed with a multitude of leather goods, mostly satchels and boots. He picked up a strange pair of dark blue leather boots. The dye was so deep it was almost black, and the designs were intricate. On the bottom was a small outline of a bird. It was too bad they cost more than both he and James made in a month.

There were fish and shellfish of every type imaginable. The meat merchant had cage after cage of chickens and geese, but there was no way their few coins would purchase something as grand as a goose—not yet anyways. Sebastian stopped and bought a few sacks of dried beans and a loaf of bread. Ah, soup it is, again.

He pushed through the crowd of people. The sounds of merchants hawking their wares and women scolding their children pushed against him like the rising heat of the summer sun. A man bumped into him and shoved Sebastian into a stall of quince, toppling over some of the golden fruits.

"What's the idea, Jack?" Sebastian whirled around but the person was gone into the crowd of market-goers. Just the top of a brown hat and bit of silver hair was visible through the crowd. Sebastian scowled the whole way back to his room, especially since he hated quince and had just purchased an arm-full.

~~~~~

The Iron Key didn't exactly look like the type of place James was used to dealing with. When in the employ of the Albrights the worst place he'd ever been to was the back room of the Sow's Ear for the occasional game of Whist. The cobwebs in the corners practically made this shop cherry. An entire wall was hung with clocks—wooden cuckoos equipped with long chains with pinecones at the ends, and others with odd symbols where the numbers ought to have been—all chiming at different times. Another wall was covered with gleaming knives and metal implements, some with hooked or jagged ends.

The tables were scattered with bizarre items, boxes and grooved metal plates that seemed almost to have a purpose, but James didn't really want to think of what that purpose might be. He picked up a small jade statue of a smiling man with his hand raised and he was sure he'd seen the figure before, perhaps in gold.

"Next!" a voice like tar called across the shop. A hunched man stood behind a basic pine counter, his face dry and flaking, and a wart growing on his cheek. He was wrapped in a brown fabric, wool most likely. His gnarled knuckles were bent around something
~~~~~

too small to see, and he slid whatever it was into a burlap sack.

James coughed, and approached the counter. "Er, are you Madoxx?"

"Who wants to know?" James was surprised by the overly typical response from the man.

"Ah, well, they call me James. But *Kellogg*"—James leaned in a bit—"told me to come by."

"Aye, I'd bet the lout did." Madoxx let out a sound James assumed was a laugh, but to him it sounded more like a chicken being mauled by a farm dog. "So, my boy, what have ye to…trade?"

James opened a black sack and placed a few items on the pine counter. Some silver forks and spoons glittered in the light of the slumped wax candle Madoxx had lit. Next to come out of James' bag were two ivory dice and a porcelain elephant.

The man glanced at the pile of silver utensils and nodded. He passed on the dice, but picked up the elephant statue.

"And what's a person to do with a porcelain pachyderm?" Madoxx croaked.

"I know the former owner kept it on a pedestal in the entry…until she gave it to me, that is."

"Aye, laddie, aye." He turned it over and squinted hard, but nodded and set it down next to the silver spoons.

Chapter 9

Over the next week, Sebastian decided he was going crazy. Not only had he thought he'd seen the silver-haired man from the coffeehouse at the market, but also at the dock while they worked to load the *Horse Dawn* for sail, and at the newest tavern Kellogg had found.

"You're just angry about the damn quince," James told him. The fruit sat in a pile on their one table growing mold. He'd refused to eat them, or let Mrs. Holding make jam out of them, or to toss them since he "broke his back to buy them damn fruits."

The following Sunday the foreman gave all the workers leave for St. Christopher's Day. With Kellogg taking his daughter Maisie to the country to visit his late wife's sister, and James nursing a hangover from the night before, Sebastian set out in the early morning to wander about before the city turned into a steam oven.

The streets were quiet. Most folks were waiting till later when the St. Christopher's Day festivities would begin. How Kellogg told it, St. Christopher appeared to a young man years ago and told him to set out by boat to a place where the coastline curves like a crescent moon. There he should build a chapel for the Lord and people will come from all around the globe to worship. And that's how they got St. Christopher's church. And the port and city sort of sprung up around it.

True or not, the people of Port City took it to heart and planned a great day in St. Christopher's honor.

He took a seat outside the coffeehouse. He watched small brown finches dart back and forth from under the eaves to the tables, pecking at crumbs of bread and begging for more. Their light whistles and chirps skittered across the small patio. Kline Hatley, the owner, set down a cup of coffee and a bun. "Are your hands green, Sketch?"

Sebastian sighed. "It's a long story, Hatley."

"I've no doubt." He laughed. A particularly fat little bird lit on Sebastian's table. "Sorry about the finches. They sure are beggars. My boy calls this one Herman," Hatley said and shooed the little bird away.

Sebastian smiled and turned to his cup. The brew was strong today, and the morning bun had just a touch of some new spice, no doubt a good deal on some spice or other had come in on the latest ship.

The fat little bird skittered back onto the table. He eyed the bun and coffee cup with a tilted head and chirped twice. Sebastian chuckled. "Ah, little friend, I think you've had enough. What will the ladies think?"

"I know who you are."

Sebastian jerked his head and saw the shape of a man outlined in the bright sun. He couldn't see the man's face.

"What's it to you?"

The man moved and Sebastian saw it was the silver-haired man. He sat down in the chair opposite Sebastian and dropped his brown hat on the table—the fat finch took flight.

"Oh, please, sit."

"Thank you."

"What do you want?"

The man with the silver hair smiled very wide. Without his hat the man's hair sprung out on all sides, grey and wiry. His suit was of a fine velveteen, like his hat. If Sebastian had thought his hair was wild, then it was nothing to how wild his grey eyes looked. He undid the top button of his burgundy overcoat and Sebastian noticed a winged ox on the clasp. "The people here call you 'Sketch,' do they not?"

"Ah, you're a good eavesdropper. But I really must leave. Merry St. Christopher's, friend." He pushed back his chair and stood.

"But you are actually Sebastian Albright."

Sebastian froze. "Do I know you?"

"I have something I believe is yours." The silver-haired man took out a plain oak box and slid it across the table to Sebastian.

"Keep your trinket box, my friend." He started to walk away from the strange man.

"They said they could smell the salt."

Sebastian spun around. "Did my father send you? Is he looking for his 'son the artist' to go home and churn out coins for his spoiled brat of a wife?" He leaned in close. "I gave that up, friend, so you go tell my father I'm done." Sebastian turned and marched away from the silver haired man, and his oak trinket box.

Kellogg told them the real festivities would happen in St. Christopher's square and he wasn't mistaken. The entire square was filled with people—jugglers and musicians, people selling food and ladies offering red flowers. At the center of the square was a tall statue of the patron saint of travelers, adorned with a bright red sash for the day.

The night was warm, on the verge of hot had the sun still been up. Most folks carried cups and fire cooked meat on sticks. A man pushed a cart along the outer square selling sweet dough fried with an aromatic seed he called anise. They weren't bad, and the scent was heady, mixing with the salty night air.

Sebastian and James took a seat at the foot of a tall column on the perimeter of St. Christopher's square. Above them was a small fountain, making the air a bit cooler than other spots. The water poured from the gruesome mouth of a smiling gargoyle or imp. Its eyes were wide and looked more surprised than fearsome.

"You knew sooner or later he'd find you." James slammed a mug into Sebastian's hand. "He's your father."

"No, he's a greedy bastard who wants a prize to show off,

like that twit he married." Sebastian tilted his cup back. "What the hell is this?"

James shrugged. "The fella selling it called it 'mead.' Said it's just like ale."

"It's horrible." Sebastian tilted his mug again. "They must have made it with seawater."

"Sorry, couldn't find any brandy carts, Sebastian." James shook his head and tilted back his own mug.

A small drum band stood at the foot of the saint's statue banging out a lively beat, and people hopped about dancing in circles. The red ribbons of St. Christopher's day fluttered from windows above, and strung from long wires crisscrossing the plaza were large banners shifting in the warm breeze. Along the main thoroughfare leading into the square, red flags were strung from lantern post to lantern post. There was no doubt tonight was a one for cheers and joy regardless how hot it still was in the night or how crowded the city had become. It was loud with voices and laughter, folks calling to friends, children running and chasing.

The moon was beginning to rise. Even with all the lantern and torch light around the square, the blue of the moon added an eerie, otherworldly look to the faces that passed by. The statue of the saint took on a heavenly glow and the gargoyle fountain a supernatural light. James' blond hair gleamed silver in the moonlight, and Sebastian did a double take, for a moment seeing the face of the silver-haired man sitting next to him on the column's base.

There was a pause in the drum music just long enough for an elderly priest standing at the foot of the saint's statue to lift up his hands and ask Saint Christopher to pray for their town, for the travelers to and from the port, and for all who travel.

At nine o'clock, the bells of St. Christopher's church began to ring out, bells pealing out a tone song that echoed down each alley and street—a flock of pigeons took flight from the bell tower.

As the bells began their festive tones, many of the people started to drift out of the square.

"Must be time for little ones to find their pillows," James offered. "Not sure they'll sleep with so much noise and music tonight." He chuckled.

The transition from night street fair to nighttime revelries was fluid. Mothers and fathers scooped their children into their arms and turned towards their doors. A father walked by with a young boy on his shoulders. The son wore a red vest and no shoes, and he waved a red flag back and forth, hitting his father's hair each time.

"Happy Saint Christopher's night!" the boy called out to Sebastian and James.

"And to you, young fellow!" James waved.

Sebastian managed to wink at the child, but turned back to his horrible mead before they were out of sight.

He shuttered and pushed himself to his feet.

"You're leaving?" James jumped up to follow.

"I'm going home."

"Oh lord, man. Why? Things are just getting going." James trotted after him.

They turned down a narrow street and had walked no more than twenty feet when yelling burst out from behind. A crowd of young men, mostly sailors from the look of them, was barreling up the street in their direction. Many of them carried torches and drums. They were merry, no doubt, but merriment and ale sometimes makes a situation more changeable than the tides.

"Oh blazes!" Sebastian shouted.

The throng was moving fast. James stood slack-jawed staring at the rowdy gang. Sebastian reached out, grabbed his collar, and yanked him back against a door. He must have used a tad too much force because the door slammed open and the two of them toppled to the floor of a shop.

"Oh perfect, Sebastian!" James rubbed his elbow. "That's gonna bruise tomorrow." Outside, the crowd of young sailors trotted past the open door. They were carrying one man who was obviously past the limit of ale a young gent can have and still walk. Poor fool was about to be waterlogged in the marina.

"Next time I'll let them trample you," Sebastian snarled, rubbing his own shoulder.

Looking around as he dusted himself off, Sebastian's eyes went immediately to a large painting on the far wall of the shop: it was the Sow's Ear, he was sure of it. The roofline was exact, the door a perfect color match—taupe and green bits showing through the chipped paint. And there was Mrs. Mac's rosebush! There was no doubt that it was the Sow's Ear.

"My God!" he thought he whispered, but had instead shouted.

"Hey!" James put a hand to his ear. "What?"

"Look, man! It's the Sow's Ear!"

James tilted his head and took a few steps towards the painting. He squinted. Sebastian's impatience grew and he tapped his foot. "Well?"

"Is that Mrs. Mac's rose?"

"Thank you!" Sebastian slapped James' back.

"Actually, her rose was more of an apothecary rose than a true rose," a man said. How he'd slipped in to stand next to them they weren't sure. But there he was, silver hair and all.

"Tell me my good man"—he turned to James—"are you aware of your friend's talent?" The strange man with the silver hair turned and walked behind a table strewn with brushes and paints. A wooden figure of a person was posed in a leaping stance. It reminded James of a puppet he'd seen years ago when some gypsies wandered through their village. The strange man's brown hat was sitting on the table next to the leaping puppet figure, and his burgundy overcoat hung off the back of a delicately carved white chair with a deep blue cushion embroidered with petite yellow flowers.

"Yes, um, he's quite good," James responded, befuddled and glancing at Sebastian.

"No, you're not."

Sebastian and James looked at each other.

"Which of us, sir?" James asked. The old man pointed at James. "You've no idea what Mr. Albright can do. And neither does he."

"Look friend, I don't know who you are, but like I told you before—leave me alone and tell my father I'll have none of this."

"You came into *my* shop."

Sebastian paused—his accusatory finger still pointed out at the old man.

"Ah, blazes!" He turned and stomped towards the open door.

"Have you ever been to the Sow's Ear, sir?" James asked.

"Oh for the love of Pete, James, let's go!"

"Once." The silver-haired man nodded. "They make a good house ale. And the proprietor's wife is quite entertaining, I must admit. Though perhaps a bit too concerned for her rosebush," he remarked offhand.

"Yes! Mrs. Mac is very protective of it!" James smiled. "Did you hear that, Sebastian?"

Sebastian stood scowling in the doorway. The night air breezed through adding the scent of salt to the dusty smell of canvas and crates. That's when he saw one—a crate with a red side, and a skinny one with a blue end.

"Those were your crates on the *Horse Dawn*?" Sebastian lunged back into the shop, pointing a hand still slightly green in the old man's direction.

"Yes, I arrived on the *Horse Dawn*. It's a good ship."

James had backed off and now passed along the walls looking at all the paintings. A small one no more than a foot square showcased a jovial looking fellow. In the background James was alarmed to see a tall tower that leaned in such a manner that only a great fool would climb to the top.

"It's a good ship?" Sebastian repeated. "That's all? How about explaining why that damn pigment came off on my hands and no one else's?" Sebastian was shouting.

"My good man"—the silver-haired old man turned to James—"what do you think of my paintings?" Sebastian threw his hands up. James' eyes went very wide, obviously hoping he'd been forgotten. "Well they are quite nice, especially this one of the man near the falling tower here. But I'm no expert, sir."

"Argento, if you please. At least that's what they called me in Firenze."

"Pah, *Argento*," Sebastian scoffed.

"Yes, *Sketch*." The silver-haired man raised an eyebrow. Sebastian's head dropped a bit and his ears went red. "And you need not be an expert, my good man." Argento turned back.

"James." He motioned to himself.

"James, talent presents itself, sometimes unwillingly, but it does."

The old man who now called himself Argento picked up an oak box.

"Oh not this again," Sebastian growled.

"What?" James asked.

Argento smiled. "Tell me, James, when your friend presented his painting to his stepmother what did the people say of it?"

James paused, his brow furrowed, unsure he should answer this man who seemed to know their story. "I remember people said it was good. And someone said they could smell salt—not that I thought that!" he added, afraid how mad that might sound, but Argento nodded.

"Oh bloody hell!" Sebastian yelled.

"Stop your protesting, Sebastian!" Argento yelled back. "You aren't fooling me. Had you not wondered what I'm about, you would have left my shop immediately." Sebastian folded his arms and sat on the carved white chair.

"Fine, *Argento*."

The silver-haired man handed Sebastian the oak box. "I believe this is yours."

Sebastian shook his head and scowled again, but curiosity took over and he opened the lid.

"Where'd you…how?"

Argento smiled.

Sebastian lifted the carved paintbrush from the box. It was shiny and polished, with the slightest tint of yellow in the grooves, and the faintest scent of dampness or earth in the bristles.

"Is that…" James trailed off.

Sebastian jumped up, knocking over the white chair, Argento's coat falling to a heap on the floor, and lunged at the old man. "Who the hell are you?" James sprang up just in time to hold his former boss back.

"I am a painter like you, Sebastian, that is all. I know real talent and you have that." Argento took him by the shoulder. "Work here and understand what I mean." His grey eyes were wide. "And I do not work for your father."

Sebastian was shaking, but inside he felt calm.

"Come back tomorrow." Argento turned and walked through a green tapestry. "And close the door behind you gentlemen," he called.

Chapter 10

The crash of the waves lingered on the sand as did the cheer of delight that rose from Maisie when she dashed away from the coming wave.

"Ye won't melt in the water, me little daisy," Kellogg called to his daughter. The girl turned about and stuck out her tongue, then skittered off back to chase the next wave.

"Such a pain in the backside." Kellogg shook his head but chuckled.

"She's funny for sure, mate," James agreed. He tossed a smooth beach stone out into the breaks.

The skies had clouded up the night before and by morning no sun could break through the cloud deck. The relief from the heat was almost instant, and instead of wasting the cool weather working, James had taken Kellogg up on his offer to join him and his daughter on the south shores. Many in Port City had the same idea and the beach was filled with picnickers and beachcombers of all ages. It was a sight to see the ladies with their dresses hitched to their knees, attempting to keep that delicate balance between fun and propriety.

Most of the waves were small with the tide out, making them perfect for young girls to run about chasing and dashing from the water's edge. Maisie's yellow dress was damp along the hem, proof that she'd not been quite quick enough, or perhaps that she hadn't cared.

"Funny maybe, but a worry to her papa for truth!" Maisie ran by kicking up the surf and splattering them both with seawater. "Ah, bullocks!" Kellogg yelled. Her laughter crashed along with the waves.

"Sketch off learning the mystical arts from that silver-haired old man?" Kellogg asked, brushing the beads of water off his trousers.

"A-course!" James yelled. "When is he not?" He flung his last beach stone high up in an arc, dropping out beyond the breaks.

"He hasn't been to the docks in a time," Kellogg remarked, eyeing the distance of James' throw. He turned his gaze down the beach where Maisie was running at a group of seagulls standing on the sand. She yelped and flapped her arms, howling as the perturbed birds took flight. She stood and gazed as the flock drifted all around her—a dot of yellow in a haze of fluttering white.

"All Sebas—erm, Sketch ever does now is paint. Don't get me wrong, he's talented. I'm telling you man, when I first saw that one painting of his, the one he complains about all the time, it was like I was standing right here, on the beach with those birds swooping and the waves and the salty smell. And it was like that every damn time I glanced at it. You know how kids can hear the ocean in a seashell?" James pointed out a little Maisie, who was skipping past a family of picnickers sitting on a checkered blanket.

"Well, that's how it felt to look at his painting. Like my ear was on a shell. Crazy, right?"

Kellogg shrugged.

"And now he's off with that old man every damn day, and the landlady wants the rent in four days or we're out."

"Lookit, Papa!" Maisie dashed up kicking sand out behind her as she ran. "Wanna bun?"

"Where the hell'd ya get that?" Kellogg looked about. Over on the picnicker's blanket, a young mother was searching through her basket for something. "Oh blazes, Maisie!" She laughed and took a bite from the bun before scampering off.

"Oh lord!" Kellogg shook his head.

"It's only a bun," James remarked.

"Today. Tomorrow, who knows."

James laughed and took a bite from the bun Maisie had handed him while Kellogg wasn't looking.

"Aye, not you too?" He laughed.

"They aren't bad, want one?" James handed him another. Kellogg sighed, then took it.

"There's a bita the thief in ya too, I'd say."

James just laughed.

They sat for a few minutes enjoying the cool breeze coming off the sea, and watching as Maisie played in the water again.

"Her mother was a good woman…She can't keep liftin'

things."

"She's only a kid. It'll pass…" James offered, but in his mind he saw the image of him and Sebastian pinching cakes from the baker's window when they were about eight, and the way Caroline's silver had glistened in the moments before it landed in his black bag.

"I don't think it will, lad. Her school mistress says she's been out on the streets with the street children. The woman called her a ragamuffin."

"And what did you call the school marm?" James laughed.

The waves crashed on. From where they sat looking north James saw Port City's docks and the multitude of ships, the masts looked tangled and interwoven from his vantage point. The chaos of the city seemed so far from them. With the birds circling and the children laughing—how could anyone feel so lost?

"Don't look so beaten, lad." Kellogg broke into James' contemplation. "What if there was a way to finish off both these odd problems at once?"

"What?"

"Look, I'm skipping town. I'll not have my little girl turning ragamuffin—or like her papa." Kellogg looked away but James saw the pain on his face. "My sister lives up north, but I haven't enough from the docks to take us home. That girl needs a country life."

"But what would you do in the country?" James questioned.

"My papa was a blacksmith, I might do that. It don't matter."

Kellogg stood and faced James. "Anythin' for me little Maisie, mate."

James watched as Kellogg's daughter spun around in the surf. Her patchwork dress was a swirl of yellow.

"How do I help?"

~~~~~

Sebastian believed the direct heat of the midday sun on the docks had to be the worst heat ever invented. After three weeks working in the silver-haired man's studio he would gladly pick the docks. The proprietor kept every window in the shop locked, and never left the shop while Sebastian was there. Even on those nights when the muse kept the young painter there until the third watch, the silver-haired man would sit at his table in his carved white chair and sketch figures or move the wooden puppet into strange poses. Sometimes he would watch as Sebastian painted, nodding silently, or shaking his head and tell him to observe the light in his mind, and think of how the shadows play in true sunlight, not the candle's flicker.

There were days when Sebastian would throw down his brush and stomp home, and others when Argento would clap him on the back and excuse him to get his rest.

All of Port City let out a unified sigh of relief on the day the clouds rolled in. While James mentioned something about the
~~~~~

beaches, Sebastian only thought of having one day when Argento's shop wouldn't feel like an oven.

Argento stood back at the edge of the room, examining Sebastian's work. Against a peach colored sky, the sun set on a grove of fruit trees. Ripe red apples speckled pale blue blankets that were spread under the wide limbs. Golden grasses rippled in a breeze, leaning against the tree trunks. A well-worn trail led off through the grove, leading somewhere unseen, where the top of a pointed roof peeked just over the horizon.

"Rare. Such talent." Argento's voice carried a combination of praise and jealousy which Sebastian heard first.

"What? What's wrong with it?" Sebastian said defensively.

Argento chuckled and strolled further into the workroom. Boxes of canvasses and paints sat in shambles against the walls, the oddly painted ends still vivid and colorful. Red and blue paint drips decorated the spot under the young painter, who held his paintbrush in one hand as he crossed his arms against his chest. His dark hair fell forward in his face and he blew it out of his eyes instead of changing from his defiant pose.

"Don't be so defensive, Mr. Albright." The old man chuckled again. Sebastian apparently didn't think it so funny as he snorted and put up his chin.

"Sebastian, understand me." He placed his hand on Sebastian's shoulder. "You possess a talent I crave. These apple trees and soft hillsides emit a truth of form I cannot convey."

Sebastian relaxed some, but only for a moment. His head tilted and he squinted at his new teacher.

"Wait. You paint people—portraits."

"Yes."

Sebastian shook his head and marched out to the front of Argento's shop where all the master's paintings hung.

Many were of people, but some were landscapes—mountains and ships on the sea, sunsets over open plains, and the large canvass of the Sow's Ear that first caught Sebastian's eye those weeks ago.

"These sure don't look like portraits to me." Sebastian posed again, this time with his arms open like an actor taking a bow.

Argento followed his student into the shop front.

"Making people is ten times harder than 'scapes," Sebastian went on, "and you've painted hands, hands are extremely difficult." He pointed to a figure of a jaunty fellow turned around in his chair, his hands folded carelessly on the back.

Argento nodded but stood silently.

"And noses!" Sebastian yelped. "I tried a painting of my father once and he looked like he'd gone five rounds with Chance Porter's flunkies!" Sebastian slumped into the carved white chair in a huff.

After a moment or two of silence, Argento went to the wall

and took down one of his smaller paintings. The cherry red glow of a bright sunrise over an old millhouse stood out in the muted light of the shop. Along the edges of the canvas, lanky ash trees stood guard, forest green leaves tending towards obsidian in the pre-dawn scene. To the left of the serene mill and home stood a rocky limestone outcropping marking the lowest point of a hillside that must rise just out of sight.

Argento presented it to Sebastian, who held the frame with respect, though confusion was playing in his eyes.

"What do you see, Sebastian?"

Sebastian raised his eyebrow when he looked at his teacher.

"A pastoral scene, a red sunrise, and trees." He paused. "Is it really a railway station?" Sebastian joked and sniggered to himself.

Argento wasn't moved. "Look again."

Sebastian walked to the window at the front of the shop, and leaned towards the grey light. He stood for a few minutes analyzing a relatively simple painting, not one of much interest except for the glowing red color, perhaps. He tilted his head to the right and something caught his eye.

It was an eye.

Sebastian snapped the painting out to arms' length and scanned it again. In the rocky limestone Sebastian now clearly saw the outline of a head, the nose had been only a raised stone, and the mouth a divot in the rock.

Each ash tree was a slim figure, as a ballet dancer mid-pirouette, and there was an unmistakable hand in the sails of the windmill.

"What on earth is this?"

Argento shrugged, changing none of Sebastian's perplexed look. Instead he merely wandered over to a piece of parchment lying on his desk and with a pencil began to sketch a building. As he added more detail Sebastian saw the facial form appearing behind the building's structure.

Argento dropped the pencil and motioned about the shop. As if walking in the mud of a river, Sebastian flowed around the room scanning each of Argento's works—now seeing the hidden faces and people in the rocks and hills and crashing waves.

"How…" Sebastian started but couldn't finish.

Argento stood beside his pupil.

"It is my curse, perhaps. I see the face in the rock," he answered like a philosopher. Sebastian turned and leaned slightly away from his tutor.

"Does this happen in all of your works?" Sebastian asked and took another step back.

"Yes."

He turned slowly and looked again at the painting of the Sow's Ear. In the twisting shrubbery of Mrs. Mac's rose bush he could see the graceful figure of a woman, as if the spirit of Mrs.

Mac's care for her plant was manifested in the greenery itself. Up on the tavern's roofline, the grain of the slopping beams rippled into the figure of a sleeping man.

"My god," Sebastian muttered. He shivered, feeling a chill for the first time since arriving in Port City. "It's…amazing."

Argento smiled and tilted his head in thanks.

"Yet not one soul has ever smelled salt when looking at my paintings."

Chapter 11

Summer's reprieve did not last long and instead returned with a vengeance. The evening sea breezes that would cool the city a little overnight disappeared, leaving residents of Port City in especially bad moods. Practically every hour there was some kind of scuffle between men over women, or women over prices, or thieves over being caught by the watch, that required the residents to peer down from their windows.

While James found respite from the heat at the tavern over ale with Kellogg most nights, Sebastian attempted to sleep through the heat one Tuesday night, on Argento's orders. But there would be no sleep. Even with a window open, it did little to stir the stifling air. And worse, his mind swam and spoke, not letting the silence of an exhausted and overheated city come to him.

There was no use—he'd never get to sleep. He let out a heavy sigh and lit the candle on the floor next to his bed. Kellogg had laughed when Sebastian took the hunk of charred plank home with him one night, but now he broke off a piece and slid it across the whitewashed walls of their room. In the last flicker of the candlelight was the image of a woman looking out into the distance over a stone wall. He sat for the next two hours shading and drawing until he finally passed out.

There was a ship much like the *Horse Dawn*, but with a green hull and masts striped in two shades of blue, swirling like a whirlpool above the deck. The ship tossed and rolled back and forth in rough seas and a storm churned off the portside. He pitched forward and was flung against the rail as a lightning bolt struck the mast. The crack of thunder shook him and he felt it rumble through him. As it rolled away, the sound of the waves faded and he looked up. He was standing on a hill, deep green in foliage, and speckled here and there with violets. Turning his head to the right—there she was. She was looking down at him and she seemed so sad. Her arms were bare and he saw the collar of her yellow dress. Her face was clear, unlike so many dreams when faces blurred into shadows.

"Anna."

He jerked awake, half out of his bed with one arm on the floor holding him up. He flung his sheet off and turned over.

"Why don't any of the bloody windows in this place open!" Sebastian shouted from the back of the studio the next night.

"This is what I wish," Argento called back.

"Crazy old fool. The hell with what you want." Sebastian flung a stool under a blue stained glass window in the ceiling. With broom in hand, the young artist banged on the latch until it creaked apart. Just enough light poured in from the full moon, not to mention the escaping heat, to appease him.

"Now I can work." He dropped off the stool and went back to his canvas.

The blue light of the window cut the image in half. Glass-light tinted a dark pine forest into midnight, while the pale moonlight tinted the lowlands and grand castle pale and eternal. A river flowed from the horizon to the foreground, dividing the landscape almost exactly at the light-line.

"Arrgh!" he growled and flung the brush to the ground.

"Please avoid my canvases when you throw things." Argento stood in the doorway with two teacups, one held out to Sebastian.

"It's too hot for tea." Sebastian scowled.

"It is not tea. It is grappa. I found a taste for it when I lived in Florence. Now pick that up. He pointed to the brush.

Sebastian shook his head but leaned and took up his brush. He dipped it into the paint. "No, that's enough tonight," Argento said while examining the painting covered in blue light. "But no artist should be so careless to his tools, Sebastian." He sipped his grappa.

"Damn! The blasted paint's on my hands again!" Sebastian drew out his handkerchief and started wiping blue paint from his right hand, to no avail.

"Is that bad? Now you wear the mark of your craft." Argento smiled.

"It just stays on so long. This paint of yours, where is it from?"

"My home."

Sebastian snorted like he always did when his tutor became

cryptic. "Of course."

"Drink, Sebastian. Sit and listen to me." He handed the younger man a cup. Blue paint smeared on the white porcelain.

Once Sebastian and he clinked cups, Argento turned a bit more serious—even for him.

"That paint, the little I have left, was made from a crushed rock we called peregrinite. It is only found in my homeland, as far as I've been able to tell, so I've been quite careful over the years to ration it to projects especially worthy."

Sebastian looked both flattered and uneasy. "I've never heard of peregrinite."

"I know." Argento took a sip of grappa. "As I was saying, almost three years ago I was living a life of relative joy. I spent my days painting and governing the township."

"Governing?" Sebastian interrupted.

"Aye. You might say I was like a duke is here, truth be told." Sebastian stared. "It isn't that grand—the castle was modest, just enough rooms for the two—"

"Castle!"

"Yes, castle."

Sebastian's eye slipped to his canvas and the grey castle he'd painted in the distance.

"In those days there was peace for the most part," Argento continued, "except for the occasional ruffian in the town alehouse.

Of course the rumors swirled of a distant relation sweeping in to challenge my place. But I have no one but my granddaughter now."

Sebastian nodded absently, "Really?"

"It is true. My wife of many years was taken by sickness. Our son died of a broken heart when his young wife didn't survive the birth of their daughter. For a time I believed only tragedy would follow me, forever," he set down his cup, "but my granddaughter brought me hope and life returned to normal."

"So why—"

"I'm telling a story, Sebastian. Let a man finish." Sebastian waved his hand. "Throughout my homeland people knew of my talent for portraits. So when I received a request from the lord of a neighboring township for a portrait for his daughter's nuptials, I made arrangements to travel…"

~~~~~~

Sand flew through the cracks in the carriage's door and window coverings. The Duke rubbed his nose and blew it hard into a linen handkerchief. He felt bad actually using it since his granddaughter had stitched his initials so neatly, but there was no helping it.

Although the Duke had pondered why his neighbor Lord Gower had sent a carriage when he had many of his own at Weldon House, he had been polite and taken his seat beside the lord's
~~~~~~

messenger. He had waved to his granddaughter as they whipped the horses into motion. She'd waved from the tower window, so that she could watch his carriage longer, she'd told him.

"Tell me, friend." The Duke turned to the Lord's messenger after putting the handkerchief in his waistcoat pocket. "Will we make it to your master's home in time?"

The messenger grinned. "Why yes, Duke Weldon, I believe we will have much time."

"I certainly hope so. Portraits are a tricky thing, and I'm sure the Lord's daughter will be even more difficult to paint if she is worrying about her wedding day's rapid approach." He turned back to the window and lifted the covering an inch. "So much sand…what route are we taking? My driver has always used the Karney Road through Milton. I'm not sure if it is faster, but the scenery is much more pleasant." While he kept chatting, he glanced at the small compass ring on his left pinky. So many nights he and his granddaughter had found their way back to Weldon House by the waterways, instead of the main road, that he'd taken to wearing it always. It was one thing for a grown man to risk the aimless wanderings of night, but quite another for a young woman.

With his handkerchief again to his nose, the Duke glanced and saw that they were no longer riding east to Gower, but were moving north.

The Lord's messenger was no longer smiling. Instead, the

brutish man had a bronze dagger in his right hand. He seemed to be studying it.

"Tell me, Duke, do you know of the place some call the Dali? I believe in your lands they call it Saltstorm Vortex? Me and my kind just call it Terry's Flat. On the streets of Belvedere, where I grew up, the street people used to tell a tale of a lonely man who wanted to give up this life and wandered into the flat never to return. Hocus pocus believed only by women folk, I'm sure, but it keeps people from ruining our plans." He placed the dagger on the carriage seat between them.

The Duke glanced back outside. The glare from the white sands of Terry's Flat made him squint, but he looked nonetheless. How strange to think that only this morning he'd been over-packing his trunks with paints and canvases, ready to create a lovely portrait of a blushing bride. And now to be on the verge of inevitable death—such change.

"I take it friend, that you are not a messenger of my friend, Lord Gower?" he said offhand.

"I am a messenger, Duke Weldon, but for someone greater." He leaned back and put his boots up on a long black box the Duke hadn't noticed earlier.

"And also a delivery man, it appears."

The messenger smiled again. "True." He picked up the dagger and the Duke flinched, hating himself for showing his fear.

But the messenger had seen. "Worry not, you'll not be hurt by me."

For a brief second, a dark shadow passed over the carriage. Outside, the Duke looked back and saw a great boulder, taller than a cottage, to be sure.

"That'll be Terry's Stone." The messenger tilted his head back in the direction of the rock.

The Duke had heard the tales of Terry's Flat, as the man called it, many times. There were times when he'd throw on his top hat and long coat and visit the local pub in the village near Weldon House. The patrons there especially loved to tell tales of men who gave up their lives in the Flat, or pretty ladies who were chased into the Flat by ruffians. One old timer said a wizard lived in a hovel at the center of the Vortex, where the only tree grew and if you stepped foot on his land he'd cast a spell on you, never to return. No one ever questioned where the stories came from if no one ever returned.

The carriage slowed, then lurched to a hard stop. Dust and sand puffed up all around and the Duke reached for his handkerchief again.

"Duke." The messenger motioned to the carriage door.

"We've reached our stop, then?" he asked, feigning politeness. The messenger only sneered.

Terry's Flat was that—flat. On every side the land flew off to the horizon and smudged along the skyline in a white haze. Wind blew a whipping, gritty sand that burned faces. To the right was a stand of boulders. At first, the Duke believed sun-glare must have damaged his sight for the rocks changed shape, slipping forward and back, up and down in a silent and rhythmic erosion and build-up—almost like the change of color from cloud-shadows on a field. He risked the pain of sun-glare and squinted at the sky. Not a single vapor cloud in the grey sky that could play a trick on an old man's eyesight, but wind and sand enough to force his head to look away and his eyes to fill with water.

"Charming day, is it not, Duke Weldon?" Sitting on one of the morphing stones was a man. He sat in a jaunty pose, like a subject sitting for a regal portrait. Yet the position of his head made it difficult for Duke Weldon to see anything under the black hood of his suede cloak.

On cue, the man swept back the hood revealing a clean-shaven head. Across his face like a mask designed for a Carnevale Ball were a multitude of diamond tattoos. Red, black, and white, the harlequin pattern stood in stark contrast to the bleached sand of the Flat. For a brief moment Duke Weldon believed that the man was sitting shirtless with his harlequin tattoo extended down from his face across his left shoulder, until the wind swept through and he realized it was but the underside of the man's cloak flung over to expose the signature pattern.

Unlike a leopard's spots or a tiger's stripes, this predator's design made him stand out from his surroundings. The pose no longer seemed like a figure for a portrait, but like an animal about to pounce, trying to stay still so as not to frighten his prey.

The stunning large diamond shapes on the cloak and the bold color of the tattoo pattern of this man's face triggered some part of the Duke's memory, but the flash of remembrance or familiarity burned out too quick for him to grasp.

"Charming may be a bit too strong a term, sir." The Duke shaded his eyes from the pattern, and the severe gaze. "Though I am intrigued by that stone you are sitting upon—remarkable."

"Yes, the morphing stones are quite the interesting phenomenon, wouldn't you say? Much like the cloudless lightning." The man in the cloak remained in his pose and only slightly lifted his hand to reference the sky. "Captain, just set that next to Duke Weldon."

The messenger put the long black box from the carriage on the ground next to the Duke's feet. The sound of grinding sand on the wooden box caused the Duke to shiver.

"I take it my Captain made you comfortable on your trip, Duke?" The tattooed man flicked his head slightly and his left hand shot up and caught the Captain's bronze dagger.

"Well, I am still alive if that is what you mean," the Duke responded, continuing with this bizarre pantomime. He regarded the messenger whose throw was dead-on—no doubt from much practice, the Duke figured.

"Quite good." The tattooed man laughed, low and intentional, down in his belly. He got up from his posed seat. His height was much more than the Duke had estimated, and his shoulders were wide under the bright cloak. As he came up to the Duke, his saunter teetered on the edge of elegant and forced.

"It would be proper now for me to introduce myself, especially since you know I already know your name, Duke Weldon."

The Duke noticed one of the man's many diamond shapes looked different than the others—a raised, white scar outlined the white diamond under the corner of his left eye. "I am Victor Knell."

The Duke thought hard, and knew the name sounded familiar, but could not place it.

"Your silence makes me think you have never heard of Victor Knell—Regent of Weldon."

"Pardon me," the Duke shouted louder than he meant to. Knell sneered, his left lip curled twisting his harlequin pattern.

"I had thought of adding the title of 'Duke' but my name shall suffice. Most peasants know my name."

"In what way do you believe you are the Regent of Weldon? You have no rights in my lands."

"Rights?" Knell laughed, this time a truthful, real laugh. "I care not who has rights to Weldon. Had rights been an issue we'd not be here in the Flat, Duke." Knell returned to sitting on the morphing stones, this time with one knee up and his left elbow propped against it. "Weldon House is, and has, many treasures."

The Duke's mind raced back to the image of his granddaughter waving good-bye and how he knew he'd never see her again.

"Ah yes," he sneered again, reading the look on Duke Weldon's face. "Such an appealing young woman. She's twenty now, I believe." Victor Knell smirked, and the Duke's jaw clenched. "Worry not, I'll not harm her. I'm no monster." He rubbed the underside of his left eye, lingering on the raised white scar.

"I will never give you Weldon," the Duke said in a calm, hushed voice.

Knell laughed again, this time it started low in his gut and burst out. "And I'd nary ask for it! When the letter surfaces—in your own hand no less," he snatched a piece of parchment from a pocket, "saying that should anything happen to you, your good friend and confidant Victor Knell should watch over Weldon, do you think any of the mourners will challenge me?"

The Duke glanced over at Knell's Captain. The messenger was leaning against the carriage, arms folded tight across his chest. "Mourners. Ah, I see." The Duke nodded.

A faint click was heard over the whistles of the sand-wind. On the handle of the bronze dagger so deftly caught by Victor Knell was now a pointed key. He stooped down, flung back his harlequin cloak, and unlocked the long black box.

"I have come to prefer a simple running-through, and here in the Flat the sands and sun would finish things. But as a rule, my Captain here believes that every trace of a person should be eliminated so there can be no possibility of others figuring out what we have done. What was it you told me, Captain?"

"A scrap is the start of a trail," the messenger recited.

"Ah yes. I took his advice seeing as his experience is more than mine."

"How wise of you, I'd say." The Duke nodded, his hands in his pockets. "As they say, experience is the best teacher." He pulled out his handkerchief to blow his nose again.

"And your death will add to the mystique of the Dali, I'm sure." Victor Knell chuckled—an expression of amusement or excitement, the Duke wasn't sure. Nor did he truly care what the man who would soon be murdering him was feeling. "In truth, in my earlier days I preferred acquisition. Take this for example." He had lifted a bright silver staff, about two feet in length, from the black box and was taking a few steps back towards the morphing rocks. "This I acquired from an alchemist who was also an artist like yourself, Duke Weldon. He claimed he had found a way to energize this staff, the Traveling Device he called it, so that any object made with the peregrinite element would change to gold!" Knell paused and glanced over at the Duke analyzing his reaction.

"Really?"Hhe feigned interest. "Fascinating. You know, I prefer those paints made with peregrinite. I actually have some in the carriage."

"I happened to know that, Duke Weldon." Knell smirked and the Duke saw his nostrils flare. He flung one side of his cloak back, revealing the brightly patterned underside yet again. "Funny, the alchemist also said that too much peregrinite at a time could be disastrous! But that's what they all say when they don't want you to try something, right?"

As if on purpose, a flash of lightning lit up the drab grey sky of the Flat.

"Captain, set this up!" Knell flung the silver staff at the messenger, who sprung forward and caught it with one hand.

It was just the moment of obscene acrobatics he needed—Duke Weldon dropped to the ground and rolled under the carriage. Before the messenger could spin around or Knell could begin shouting orders, the Duke was atop the carriage in the rumble seat whipping the horses into motion. The driver was knocked out cold on the white sands.

Duke Weldon risked a look back only to see Knell in a full run to catch up with the carriage, flashy cloak snapping against his back, patterned face contorted in exertion, and his captain not far behind running with the silver staff still in one hand. The Duke flicked the reins harder and the horses obeyed, but not before Knell made a flying leap onto the back of the carriage. The messenger threw the pole like a javelin and Knell's deft hand caught it even as the carriage hit a rock.

The Duke heard the messenger yelling, "leave it, leave it, sir!" and Knell took his Captain's advice by shoving the pole into a tear in the carriage's canvas side. When he looked back, the Duke saw Knell leap down into a roll and land safely near the captain. Even as he was pulling away from them, he could see the bright red, black, and white of Knell's face and matching cloak. And then the lightning struck him.

"The afterlife is darker than I imagined…" he mumbled and put hands to his eyes, yet the dimness remained. Where had the wind gone? And the dry salt smell instead was spice and smoke. Blood pulsed in his ears, thudded like hoof beats.

"If only I had learned Italian, my friend."

The Duke twisted his head around towards the voice, realizing he had been staring at a floor. All around the face looking down on him was a halo of yellow farm light, like summer straw. Clear blue eyes stared out from a face both wise and distracted. Clearly Victor Knell with his harlequin patterned face and matching cloak and shifting stone throne had caught him after the lightning hit and this goon of his was going to kill him.

The gazing man shifted his weight to the right, revealing a ceiling of wooden beams and a row of stained-glass windows behind him.

"I would tell you not to worry. I'm not sure how much that would help, but at least you would have a friendly soul to speak to about your problems. Which by the look on your face—and that mess of a carriage in front of the church—are quite great. But alas, my Italian is very little, so, ahem: arrivederci e stammi bene…argento uomo!"

"What was that last bit, sir?"

"Oh my, you speak English?"

The Duke squinted. "I believe I do."

He sat up and peered at his surroundings. Instead of a dim afterlife, he seemed to be sitting in a small church. Candles flickered on the altar and around the perimeter. He saw statues posed with kindness and others in agony. A figure of a woman in a blue cloak, her arms low and outstretched stood to one side, and offerings of roses were placed at her feet. Light from upper windows cast down on the pair of men in an ethereal way.

"My apologies. I believed you to be a native, though your dress does remind me of home, I must admit." He was in his mid-life with a fine suit much like that of Duke Weldon's. In the dim light of the church it was difficult to see if his hair was still youthful blonde or saged grey—but judging by the age of this talkative man the Duke decided on the latter.

"Where are you from?"

The Duke hesitated.

He had been on the carriage. No, it was grassy, or was it sand? The flash and wind…

I'm from a grey salt flat where rocks move and a tattooed bastard in an overtly patterned cloak and his henchman intend to hurt my granddaughter and steal my lands, he thought. His compass was moving in slow deliberate clockwise motion.

"Wherever I am from is obviously not where I am…"

"Sorry?"

"Are you familiar with Weldon House?" he offered.

The other man looked pensive, one finger to his eye, strikingly like Knell. "That's in Shropshire, isn't it?"

"I do not believe so, no." He gripped his forehead.

"Come, let us get you some water, or as they say here in the land of the Medici—acqua!"

Summer sun, bright like gold, blinded him almost as much as the glare of Terry's Flat. The dapper man led him to an open field slightly downhill from the doorway of the church. The Duke watched his footing mostly since the dizziness had not subsided. He was warm, so much so that he peeled off his overcoat. As he flung it over his shoulder, in a motion eerily like Knell flinging his cloak, he raised his head to the warm sunlight. The sight of a deep blue river and vast city struck him so that he stopped mid-step.

"The view from here is unequaled, would you not agree?"

his companion stated, gazing across the sparkling river at the massive cathedral, its monumental dome dominating the view. Orange tile roofs and earth-toned walls blended into a color so very like that of the dried grasses of the hillsides that the city and hills were like one large swipe of his paintbrush. Faint sounds of carts and horses on cobbled streets wafted over the river and up the hillside, or maybe the Duke only thought they did.

"Here, sir, drink. Happy days!" The Duke gladly took the water, yet kept his eyes on the city below as he drank. But his companion had turned away from the view and to a chair and easel set-up on the hill, under a sweeping oak.

"Last year, I told myself, 'Joseph, go see Italy, again. See Rome and the floating city, and especially Florence.' So here I am," he continued on. "Rome was beautiful, truly the Eternal City, they say. And Venice, who can deny the splendor and exotic flair of St. Mark's? Or the way the evening light stretches on the canals?" He sighed and took out a bottle of some liquor from the satchel sitting against the chair. For the briefest of seconds, the Duke saw brushes stowed inside.

"But I must say, there is something purposeful about Florence," he continued after sipping from the bottle. "The idea that the artists I studied at the Academy walked the streets here and their pieces stand here. Why the Master himself is said to have walked these hills! It's said by the monks that the Master called this little church," he motioned back to the one they had just left, "la bella villanelle." The Duke shook his head. "Ah, that means 'beautiful country lass.' Or so I'm told," he laughed.

"That sounds quite nice." the Duke nodded, and wondered who this Master was he spoke of.

"Yes. So I set up my canvas and paints and attempt to see what the others have seen and create it in my own way. Would you care to see?"

"Yes, sir."

"The name is Turner, sir. And you strike me as a man who would prefer to keep your name to yourself."

The Duke thought about laughing, but changed his mind. "You have seen the truth of me, I would say."

"That is an artist's job, to see truth and attempt to convey it. What may I call you then?"

The Duke thought. "You called me something in the chapel—arg…"

"Argento? I was joking—it means 'silver' here. Your hair in the dim light practically glowed like one of the candles."

The Duke smiled. "I like it well enough."

"Happy to meet you then, Argento."

Turner's canvass was swept in color, yet buildings of the city stood in soft accuracy. The painting was unfinished, but the Duke could see it would be a fine representation of the beautiful city.

Turner had captured the subtlety of the day's light, and punctuated his painting with clear impressions of the sun's reflective glow.

"It is wonderful. A great representation of the landscape." He nodded and breathed a heavy sigh.

"You say that because you are envious."

The newly christened Argento was startled. "I beg your pardon."

"Oh please, no, I mean nothing rude. It is just that you are a portrait painter and you sometimes think that the landscape eludes you." Turner stooped down and pulled a black portfolio from the satchel, as Argento stood agape. "Believe me sir, I too have attempted portraits, and other than a somewhat decent self-portrait, they are not where my strength lies. Which is why I tend to the land and sea for my subjects. It seems we are on different ends, skill-wise." He handed the Duke his portfolio. In it were sketches of various buildings, many in the same style as the massive Cathedral down below.

"How did you know I am a painter?" he asked as he flipped through the portfolio.

"Your carriage is full of paints and canvases and the like. Also, you have old paint stains on your shirtsleeves and your overcoat. We are a messy bunch sometimes, are we not?" Turner smiled and sipped again from his bottle. The Duke remembered the carriage and saw it a short distance off, toppled and missing the horses, but not in the worse condition. Odd that it hadn't been burned from the lightning, he thought. Though odd didn't seem enough of a description of what was going on. He continued to page through Turner's work but stopped at a somewhat older sketch.

"Where is this one?" Argento's hand trembled.

Turner glanced at the sketch.

"That was done while I was at Oxford visiting family. The building itself is not one that is actually built there, no. It was something I was inspired to draw. But I've never painted it. I'm not quite happy with it yet. There is just something missing." Turner's brow was knitted when he took another sip. "You understand what I mean, do you not?"

The Duke understood what Turner, this strange man with straw hair who paints in a magnificent city he'd never heard of or seen the likes of before, was talking about. He understood quite well, since the sketch was Weldon House.

But worse of all was the blurry image of a girl looking out from the tower window, and the faint harlequin pattern on the man standing next to her.

Chapter 12

Sebastian sat dumbfounded.

"Turner's sketch was my first clue. Whatever the old apothecary had told Knell about gold, the staff really did amplify the process. When forced, the peregrinite can trigger and move us, but the destination is questionable. Unfortunately, only Knell's staff had a way to choose a destination. But I believe there is another way: that when crafted, the peregrinite can be used and the destination controlled."

"I…what?"

"You see, this is why I need you, Sebastian. You must make a painting so real it will let someone go to my homeland." Argento pulled back the velvet curtain, and Sebastian jumped from his stool, knocking it over. "Really, son, try to stop knocking things over." Argento shook his head and sighed.

A painting of a young woman hung on the wall. With her arms resting on her lap and a wooden staff across her left shoulder, her pose was regal. Yet her clothes were that of a peasant. Her curls hung free, a yellow band along her brow line. She looked out from the painting with such clarity.

In the distance, a small cart track wound into the hills, and a church stood melted into the low cloud cover that hugged the red hills. Those hills rolled down to a port where points of light glowed from windows and street lanterns.

"Sebastian, I believe you know my granddaughter: Annalisa Lenore."

Sebastian opened his mouth and nothing came out, a first for sure.

"What do you notice about this painting?" Argento had turned into a teacher again.

"Are you joking?"

"No."

Sebastian spread his arms. "You mean other than the fact that this is a painting of a woman I met only this spring and you think she is your granddaughter—*from a land of paintings?*" Argento nodded as if he had asked him to recite the Magna Carta.

"It's Spain." Sebastian gave in.

"Yes, and?"

"And…"

Argento squinted. "Do you hear the water? Smell the spices of the food or merchant ships?" Sebastian looked away and closed his eyes. Smells of must and oils hit his nose, smells he usually blocked out, but there was no spice. And for once he heard no waves. Even this far from the docks, at night you could hear waves everywhere in the city when breezes swept up in the evenings.

"That was when I knew I would not be able to help her," Argento said and sat on the stool.

"That was you? The man doing penance?" Sebastian marveled.

Argento nodded. "I kept my face hidden from her, the less she knew about my fate, the less Knell could hurt her, I figured. This also meant I was able to find out little of how she came to this side other than her being shipwrecked."

"Some nuns saved her," Sebastian said absently.

"Yes." He gazed at Anna's portrait. "This was my second clue. I used peregrinite to paint her portrait. I thought that if I painted her, she may end up back in our world, but I was wrong."

"Wait, send her back? After what you told me about that, that Knell guy with the tattoos on his face?" He felt like a fool even saying it.

"Anna must have escaped him or she wouldn't have ended up here," Argento reasoned. "Besides, she needed to be home in our lands: the other side of the paintings."

"You are mad!" Sebastian yelled and turned for the door. *Why didn't she tell me?* he wondered.

"It doesn't matter because she is already there!" Argento yelled after him.

Sebastian paused. "What do you mean?"

Argento walked to his carved white desk and pulled out a black portfolio from under the piles of sketches. He flipped it open and passed it to Sebastian.

There was a stone wall with an arched window. A woman dressed in yellow looking down. Leaning against the window was a carved wooden staff. And in the shadows was a tall figure with his hand on the window's ledge to the woman's left—a harlequin pattern of red, white, and black draped across his arm.

~~~~~

He had been there that first night. Her head still throbbed from the beating his henchmen delivered, her bruises forming deep blue on her arms, and her mind was fuzzy. She'd staggered to the window and seen the truth: she was back in Weldon. Through the haze of her spinning head she saw the river and the woods, the mountains far off. She could hear frogs croaking in the moat below. She was home—somehow. He'd stood close behind her at the window, holding her walking staff which he took with him when he left her alone in the locked room.

As her mind cleared, she began to remember some of what had happened. She remembered how distracted she'd been as she walked down the road away from Albright Manor—her mind had been making a plan to find Sebastian. No amount of threats from Mrs. Albright was going to keep her from her young artist. Reliving the events of the prior months, she had walked the country road thinking of the moments they'd spent by the river and in the fields, the way he smiled and the beautiful sketches he'd made. His arms
~~~~~

around her. She had been thinking of the dark hours she spent by candlelight carving the willow-wood coin for him, and remembering how Sebastian's blue eyes with flecks of grey stared back into hers with a look that needed no words. That was when the man had grabbed her walking staff and beat her over the head. One of her kidnappers had said something about a traveling device, and another had said peregrinite, before she'd seen a bright flash like lightning. She awoke to a voice saying, "Welcome home, Lady Weldon." The shock had left her dizzy, but she could see the red, white, and black patchwork of diamonds on her captor's face.

Knell had gotten his way, her supposed disobedience now punished—Anna was back at Weldon House.

After a day or two, she wasn't sure really, she could feel the fogginess begin to recede like clouds on the coastline. Anna tried to stand but the ringing in her ears and the throbbing of the bump on the back of her head the size of an egg forced her back to the edge of the bed. She took a slow deep breath, then rose slowly and stumbled to the window. She felt haze on the edge of understanding, from her bout with the traveling device, no doubt.

Weldon. How could it be? Outside were the lands she knew, the river, the woods, the mountains in the distance. So like the Albright Manor, yet not. Like a spark or a simmer Anna could feel the fogginess trying to dissipate, though her head still pounded. Her breath came slow and with purpose, stilling the confusion. The far-off sound of river water played to her ears, so much like the waves hitting the sides of the ship. On the *Pegasus* she'd stood on the deck, amazed by the sea's vastness and beautiful blue-green waters. The captain had told her to go below deck. She'd watched the storm approaching on the horizon and noticed the blue haze of peregrinite dust from the mines on her skirt begin to glow.

And then there was a flash of lightning…

She groaned and reached a hand up to her forehead. Her pulse beat along her temples, drowning out the memory of the shipwreck. Anna's eyes wobbled a bit so she leaned against the tower room's windowsill. Agan, she inhaled slowly. This was not the return to Weldon she'd imagined.

In Spain, when the brothers at the monastery had shown her an atlas of the known world, Weldon wasn't there. Perhaps it was too small, one brother had kindly offered. She'd nodded in politeness, but wondered at the dragons on the edges of his maps. They also had never heard of peregrinite; it wasn't a mineral listed in any of their books. Though she had it on her clothes before she'd been shipwrecked.

There had been a wall in Colina Roja's small chapel with a beautiful mural that looked familiar, like an image from her past. She asked of the artist and one of the brothers said it was done by a man on a journey, they didn't know his name or where he was from. At the time she'd thought it a lovely coincidence. Soon after that she'd boarded a ship to England in search of—

Grandad.

"Oh my God!" she shouted to the room. "He was him, the man, the one who was to pay my fare to England! Why didn't he tell me?" She realized how loud she was shouting when two doves took flight outside the window.

She squinted out to watch them fly, though it made her stomach turn to move that fast, and saw the distant crossing bridge downriver that she'd used to escape Weldon before, like a smudge on a painting.

"Sebastian," she said again, and drew her breath back in sharply.

His paintings seemed so real, everyone said it. The guests said they could hear waves crashing.

She slammed her fist on the windowsill. *Dammit all! He must think I ran off. Maybe even lied to him about everything…Which I guess I did, a bit, oh God,* her mind was racing. *And Grandad is alive! Where could he be? Why didn't he tell me?*

She focused on the smudge of the crossing bridge downstream.

Victor Knell.

"Of course," she said out loud. "If the peregrinite worked on the traveling device, like the raw dust on my skirts in that storm…" Her agitation won out over the headache. She was speaking in broken phrases. Memories flashed, thoughts simmered and burst out from her mind.

"If he was over there, and I was there–but *what* is there?" She wiped her forehead and caught a glance of the bruise on her arm. She stopped short.

"Oh lord, does *he* know?" Anna's head swiveled slowly towards the locked door to her tower prison. *No, he must not,* she thought. Her heart was racing.

"He'd have killed him," she whispered.

~~~~~

There had been a time, long ago, when Victor Knell led by perfect example: he helped the elderly washer woman with her basket; he dropped gold coins in the musician's hat; and he devised peaceful trade agreements with the tenant farmers in the outlying family lands.

As summer waned in Knell's twenty-first year, harvest reports were promising—the wheat and barley of the tenants should be a bumper crop, and the grapes were almost ready to pick.

Victor's ailing father always enjoyed reading the harvest reports each year. Since the Elder Knell had gone into the twilight state, he hardly reacted anymore. But his eyes would sparkle when Victor told him about the wheat and grains and the Fall plantings.

Until the day they didn't. The doctors were called, and then
~~~~~

the priest, and then the undertaker.

And then there was the lawyer.

It was more than a love of harvest time that Victor's father had cherished. Upon his death, all the tenants were to be given ownership of their plots—all three hundred of them.

All that would remain for the younger Knell was the family estate, a few acres surrounded by former family lands. Victor stood and looked out over the empty wheat fields, stripped of the rewarding harvest, a barren promising look.

He started by having the lawyer killed—no one noticed. With him gone and his father's will still not publicly read, he hired a local man to modify the dates. A new lawyer declared the original a forgery and Victor inherited the family lands.

That's when the grumbling began.

Most had known they would own the lands they worked someday, and no amount of gold coins dropped in hats could change the tenants' opinions of a petty boy who wanted what wasn't his. So Knell lowered his payments to the farmers, and dispatched the ones who continued to rebel. On one farm, the peasant was particularly disobedient, claiming the Elder Knell would never have treated them such.

That was the first time Victor killed a man.

Standing against the mantle in his room, a roaring fire in the grate, Victor shook, quivered. He swore he could feel his organs rattling in his gullet.

He reached for a quill off his father's former desk and jabbed the point into his skin. Blood mingled with the black ink. His fist gripped the pen tight, and with the control of a surgeon he carved a diamond under his left eye.

Was it instinct that moved his hand? And why the diamond? Victor's brain was vibrating and swirling in new ways and couldn't give him an answer, other than it was right. He knew this diamond was more than a cut, it was meaning and truth and identity—and it was perfect.

Ink and blood ran like tears down his cheek—black tar, melded with slick crimson. Sometime later he paid a traveling mystic to fill in the livid white diamond scar with permanent white ink.

And now, fifteen years on, a face masked in black, red, and white diamonds, Victor Knell was calling himself Regent of Weldon House. When that disobedient girl had escaped him there was no question he would have her found, locked in her tower room to stare out at the lands that could have been theirs.

And he did. She had returned a failure.

Chapter 13

"No change?" James scowled at the barkeep.

"Nay, ya owe for last night, too."

"Bah! I paid ya." James blinked and swayed where he stood.

Kellogg glanced at James from his seat in the back of the tavern. He shook his head and sipped his ale. It wasn't very good, and he didn't want to get too drunk tonight. He needed his ears more than his muscles he figured.

Two tables over, next to one with a man passed out in a puddle of his own drool, sat Chance Porter. His back was to Kellogg, but that was all fine considering he needed to watch the lips of the little man sitting next to Porter, in case he couldn't hear his actual words.

"It's either tonight or never, Porter," the little man said. "Silver'll be gone tomorrow. The owner is sick of all this blasted heat." He took a swig of his ale. His mug seemed twice the size of a normal one in his small hands. "I heard he's making for Scotland on the morrow."

Porter leaned back. Kellogg turned back to James who had just yelled something about helping out a friend.

"Midnight then, lads. In, out, off to Carington to meet next Thursday." Porter slammed down a mug and one of his mates did the same. Kellogg saw he had a ratty bandage around his hand, then noticed that Porter was the only one who had a cushion on his chair.

"Hand me ma coins, man!" James' voice became loud, almost as loud as the guitar player's tunes. That was enough.

"All right, what's say we walk?" Kellogg's hand slapped James' shoulder and he slumped back onto the barstool. "Com'on—up!" He hoisted James to his feet.

Outside, James stood at the corner of the alehouse crouched over making retching noises as people went by.

"Ah, one too many, my friend!" Kellogg boomed and laughed with the passers-by.

"Ok, don't make me look too lame," James whispered from his awkward position.

Kellogg chuckled. "All part of the show, mate." James shook his head, but made a few more noises as a sailor passed.

"Like daughter, like father, eh?"

"Where'd ya think Maisie learned it?" Kellogg beamed. "So Porter and his crew are moving on it at midnight. I'd say we move now—that is after you're done with your show here. Gotta make sure word spreads inside that a man is sick out here."

"Wait, you want to go now? What about Seb—Sketch. I thought—"

"You want that silver, or do you want to wait three days for the moody git to ponder?"

James glanced towards the docks. "No, I guess not, but what

about—"

"No worries, Gimp, ya still get half." Kellogg put out his hand.

"Let's go then." James shook his hand.

The shipment of silver had been stored in the back of a dank warehouse at the far end of the wharf. James hadn't ventured this far down the docks even in daylight, and having his first trek in the 10 o'clock hour was not what he had hoped. Pinching silverware from the Albright's kitchen had been much simpler, he thought, and he couldn't remember feeling this jumpy when he stuffed that porcelain elephant into his bag. Sylvia had even caught him as she limped off to the sheep pens that morning. He remembered how swollen her eyes had been when she nodded at him and limped passed.

"Hey!" Kellogg smacked his arm. "Ya with me, mate?"

"Yeah, I'm with you," James snapped back.

Kellogg had broken the lock and was three steps inside before James followed. They crept along, weaving around tall crates and stacks of ship-building planks. Above, along the top of the warehouse walls, were open shutters that let in the moonlight. James sniffed and choked on the wet seaweed smell mixed with mold or old rotted wood.

"Ah, here we are." Kellogg tromped over to a small box marked "Bhaltair." He pried open the top plank. Inside, mixed with dry blond straw, was a pile of braided silver chains. To James, the silver shone like white fire in the pale moonlight. After being tossed about on the ship, the strands had become tangled, so Kellogg and James grabbed handfuls. Kellogg grinned as he dropped the chains into a burlap sack, and James shoved his fire-white silver into the black bag that once held Caroline's elephant.

"That's all of it, looks like." James sifted his hands through the straw.

"Then let's get!" Kellogg smiled and clapped him on the back, then bounded for the door. James scrambled to follow as he tied up the black bag. He took another look behind him at the empty crate and spun 'round just in time to stutter to a stop without running into Kellogg.

That was when the match was struck.

"Kellogg, ya really shoulda used a better decoy. This one's not even as good as yer little girl." Chance Porter pointed at James. Chance was flanked by his crew, including the one with the bandaged hand and one with the remnants of the shiner Sebastian gave him.

Porter's man dropped a scrap of yellow cloth to the ground—it was a kerchief.

"She told me her papa would smash my head in when he found me." Chance Porter took a step forward. "Of course that was after she stomped my foot and sucker punched Vergil here in the gut." Kellogg's eyes went very wide, but even in his fear there was a twinkle of pride. "So Kellogg, think you'll be punchin' in my head tonight?"

He laughed. "Ah, my Maisie always was a keen one." He laughed again and cocked his head to the side—then swung his burlap sack round right into the side of Chance Porter's head.

James and Kellogg jolted off down the dock.

"Lads!" Porter was yelling and they heard his men running after them.

"I thought," James got out as he ran, "ya said midnight?" They darted left down a ramp and onto the main docks.

"They did!" Kellogg jumped a crate more dexterously than James would have figured he could. "They was playing us like we were them." They ducked behind a large cluster of crates that smelled of old fish. James gagged and tried to get his breath back.

"My God! Maisie! I gotta get her!" Kellogg grabbed James' collar. His fear was electric and primal.

James hesitated. In the distance they heard angry voices and boxes being smashed to bits—obviously one of Porter's gang was handy with a hammer.

Kellogg looked so desperate and vulnerable. James had thought there was nothing in this world that could have scared the stocky dock-worker. It was unsettling and raw.

"Go, man. I'll try and distract them. I've seen how Maisie does it." James tried to smile.

He let go of James' collar. "Thank ya, man," his voice was like gravel. "Truly."

With his black bag in hand, James stood and peered back along the wharf. One of Porter's men, the one with the hammer, was only a few hundred yards off.

"James!" Kellogg hissed. "Ya tell Sketch I say bollocks on old man Albright."

"What?" James said a bit too loud since the footfalls of Porter's man suddenly sped up.

"And you two look me and Maisie up if you ever find yourselves in Maytonshire."

With a final nod at Kellogg, James leapt out and started running, swinging the bag of silver into the crates as he went.

"Hey! There they are!" the man yelled and started after James. His fellow joined in the chase only feet behind.

After Porter's men stomped past, Kellogg crept out from behind the crates. Far off, the bright moonlight was shining off James' blonde hair. "That's why Maisie wears her kerchief," Kellogg whispered to himself. "Papa's coming, Maisie-girl."

~~~~~

The echo from him slamming Argento's shop door followed Sebastian down the street, fading away only as he marched around the corner.
~~~~~

"Ridiculous!" he muttered. "He's mad." Sebastian pounded his fist on the top of a wooden barrel as he passed. He dragged his sleeve across his brow and continued his march to the wharf.

At the beginning of the breakwater, he jumped over a pile of ratty canvas and rope that in the moonlight were bright white. "The thought!" he exclaimed to no one, and let out a growl of frustration.

Sebastian plopped down on a crate, just far enough out on the breakwater so that the smell of rotted fish was overpowered by the fresh salt air. He looked out at the eastern curve of the bay. Flecks of light from homes scattered across the dark city, and beyond that was just the hillsides and green, open fields.

"She wore a yellow dress..." Sebastian's wild dream slammed back into focus. "In that tower thing, she was wearing yellow and she looked so...sad." He remembered the image of her gazing down at him from so high, and he saw her face.

"But there was no man in a harlequin pattern in my dream!" he argued back. "That proves it, my friend." Sebastian pounded his fist on the side of the crate. Then his shoulders slumped. "Proves I'm just as mad, I think."

He let out another of his growls and put his head in his hands.

From off in the distance, a scuffling rose up, or was it a drummer? Sebastian uncovered one eye and caught a flicker of light bouncing up the wharf.

"Ha, looks like someone's been caught with the foreman's

wife again," he chuckled and was about to resume his eye-covered pose when he realized the light was really the reflection off someone's hair. Someone's blonde hair.

"Oh for the love of Pete!" Sebastian jumped up and dashed up the breakwater.

He reached the docks just as James ran by like a madman escaping the asylum.

"What the hell's going on!"

James stumbled at the sight of him. "Sebastian? Oh God, no time. We have to—"

A loud splintering crash cut James mid-sentence.

"Come on! It's Porter." He grabbed Sebastian by the arm and started running again.

"Porter?" Sebastian was still looking behind them. "What the hell does—" Another smash broke out and Sebastian took off after his friend.

"All right, out with it," Sebastian said when he'd caught up around the next corner.

James glanced around and ducked into an alleyway. "They have Kellogg's little girl," James said between shuttering breaths. "It was the only way Kellogg could go after her."

Sebastian scratched his head. "My God! But why? Why are Porter's men after Kellogg and you in the first place?"

James looked down the alleyway again and pulled the strings

on his black bag. He tilted it so the moonlight shone on the contents. The braided bands of heavy silver shone so bright that Sebastian squinted. "Is that…"

"Yes."

"James."

James yanked the bag closed. "Not all of us get to sit around and paint all day, sir."

Sebastian opened his mouth to protest, but decided against it. "Then I guess you had no choice. Someone had to help Maisie."

James nodded and peaked around the wall.

"Wait, if Porter was able to get to Maisie, then they know where they live, which means they might know where we live too," Sebastian said. "We can't go back there."

James let out a snort. "Well, great! Then where the hell do we go?"

Sebastian tilted his head and shook it at his thieving friend.

Chapter 14

"Argento!" Sebastian called as he and James burst through the shop door, slamming it hard against the wall and knocking a painting of a boy and his yellow dog off the wall.

The shop was dark, but Sebastian stumbled forward, easily dodging his teacher's desk. "Argento!" he yelled again. James picked up the small painting from the floor.

"Perhaps you should bolt the door after you've hung up my painting, James." Argento appeared from the back studio with a lantern in hand. "Don't look so confused, Sebastian. I know the look of young men who have gotten into too much trouble. My hair was not always so silver."

James slid the bolt.

"Now, do you mind telling me why you two have burst in so? Though it does seem all too familiar." Argento chuckled as he sat down in his carved white chair.

"Well, my friend here," Sebastian said as he marched past him and into the back studio, "just *may* have stolen some goods, and just *may* be running from the local scoundrel." He lit another lantern and started sifting through papers and shuffling around.

"Ah." Argento looked away from his pupil and turned to James, whose ears were growing red. "So, you have joined the ranks of those skilled in legerdemain?" James looked around at the walls.

"Or perhaps this is not quite your first foray into the art?"

"Well…"

Sebastian froze with a jar of paint in one hand. He turned and walked slowly back out to the main room.

"James, is he right?"

James bounced on his toes, "I may have pinched some things in the past, it's true."

"Oh blazes!"

The black bag dropped to the floor with a thud and clink of metal. "Don't you judge me, *Master Albright!*" James was inches from his former boss' face. "You may have hated your father, but you never had to struggle a day for food. Even here, you didn't. So I lifted some of Caroline's silver and a few other things from back home. It just meant we didn't starve in a city where you left your name behind, *Master Albright.*" James bowed, arms spread mockingly.

Sebastian's fist connected with James' nose before he even knew he'd moved. With James sprawled out on the floor, Sebastian was yelling over him, "Damn you, James, you son of a bitch!"

Sebastian lifted his fist again and lunged, but Argento jumped up from his seat at his desk and held him back.

Sebastian's knuckles were bleeding like James' nose.

"Oh, very classy, sir." James got to his feet and flung blood from his nose to the floor.

"You idiot! Why would you steal back home?"

"All you ever saw of our life was Three Oaks, the ale and the maids, and that Anna girl," James yelled. Argento handed him a handkerchief. "It was harder then you knew."

Outside a window shattered.

"Hell, it's Porter. We have to hide." Sebastian marched off to the back studio. He stood under the blue skylight and rummaged around under the crates.

"I believe you are looking for this." Argento stood next to the far wall. A cellar door was opened in the floor with a lavish oriental rug kicked out of the way. "Gentlemen, after you."

Three steps down into the root cellar and the temperature had already dropped by ten degrees. Brown flat stones, feet wide, made up the floor. The wooden beams of the shop floor hung over their heads. With a lantern glowing bright, Argento moved across to the far side where two more lanterns waited to be lit. Boxes painted varying colors were stacked up neatly on the stone floor.

As Argento lit the remaining lanterns, Sebastian realized that the temperature was even cooler than he thought.

"Your new painting's very good," James grumbled through the bloody handkerchief and Sebastian turned around. His painting of the castle next to the pine forest was sitting between the two lit lanterns.

"What is that doing down here?" He scowled. Argento raised

an eyebrow and glanced at James. "Oh, um, thanks, mate," Sebastian mumbled.

"It is down here for its protection. I did not want a gateway to be left exposed, even in the back of the shop."

"Gateway?" James asked, still pinching his bloody nose.

"Don't listen…it's nothing," Sebastian said and shivered.

James nodded, then thought better of it, but glanced at the floor. "Is that my satchel? And that's yours…"

"Yes, you will need your things." Argento picked up a third bag and Sebastian realized that his teacher was wearing his burgundy overcoat and held his brown hat in one hand. "I had hoped we would leave tomorrow after your head had cooled a bit, but we need to go now, else this Porter chap may find you both," he said as he pulled on a brown leather glove with a small bird embossed on the cuff.

James looked utterly confused, his throbbing nose didn't help any.

"Look, even if I did believe you, which I don't, how the hell do we go *through* a painting?" Sebastian asked.

"Wait, *through* a…" James trailed off, his eyes wide.

Argento handed each of them their bags. "You, my friend, are the painter, and this is your painting—make it happen."

Sebastian stared at the painting. Lantern light cast a yellow glow around the edges of the dark forest and pale castle. James jumped. "Did you hear an owl? Are there owls in the city?" Argento shook his head. "You must have rattled my head pretty damn hard, Sebastian." James was rambling.

A loud crash came from upstairs.

"You heard that, right?" James asked and Argento nodded. "Damn, they found us!" James whispered.

Sebastian looked at his friend—bloody nose, a bag of stolen silver in one hand, his personal things in the other—then back at the painting. "Here's hoping that Porter's men will have pity on three mad men…" He stood back from his painting, closed his eyes, and jumped.

Chapter 15

He lay sprawled against a moss-covered log. The decaying wood perfected soft soil and nurtured the saplings sprouting between moss and mushroom. He was oblivious to the cold and damp, to the beady eyes of the clearing residents that investigated the stranger. Twitching noses sniffed his slumped hands; curious paws tapped his bare legs and jumped back waiting for retaliation.

A gust shook the undergrowth sending most residents scurrying back to their holes. The rest bolted when the stranger stirred.

The echoes above swirled through the tree branches grating and sheering in his ears. Like in a grand temple, intoning voices of holy men speaking of life and spirit…or death and beyond.

The hollow questioning of owls peering out from their nests in the tall pines added to the dreamlike, other-worldly feel of the forest. "Who?" they questioned the strangers that had appeared in the glade.

"How the hell do I know?" Sebastian mumbled.

As if in response, the inquisitive bird dove from its hollow nest and glided over the impertinent stranger; flapping its tawny wings enough to ruffle his damp hair as it passed.

"When...ere'm I?" he slurred, opening only one eye and taking in only darkness. The smell of damp leaves and moss crept into his nose.

He sat up like a spring toy when the lever is snapped.

"Oh great God…"

The oppressive heat of Port City had been replaced by a cold only describable as knives carving into ice. His whole body ached. Every muscle and joint screamed. Grime and wet dirt clung to his pants and hands.

Across a small empty space covered in pine needles was another tumbled log that was growing frilly white mushrooms on one end. Sebastian was reminded of the fancy dinner plates Caroline insisted be used when guests came. On the opposite end of the log, the wild silver hair of his mentor glowed in the low blue light.

Rising up to one knee, Sebastian grabbed his forehead and plopped back to the damp ground. The pressure between his ears pulsed, and he felt his eyes in their sockets.

"Oh, for the love of Pete!" he mumbled.

"The pain won't last but a few minutes, an hour at most," Argento said. Sebastian grumbled something, but stopped short when Argento flung a heavy cloth at him. The wool was scratchy in places, but there was a familiar smell—hay and oak mixed with linseed. It was his coat from home. The deep navy blue came from the best dyes his father could purchase. Of course it was never worn by royalty or gypsies like other over-garments.

Sebastian got to his feet on his second attempt but swayed a bit.

The pine branches above slammed and swayed against each other, creating a sound like tides against docks or a river crashing in white-water breaks over boulders. The frigid air seeped into each quarter inch of his exposed skin and he growled in response. Sebastian swung the woolen coat over his shoulders as he growled against the winds.

As if in response to Sebastian's grumbling, another gust swept through the grove, flinging his damp hair into his eyes. The wind screeched in the branches. It was like a hollow scream, staggering between elation and pure fear.

"Where's James?"

Argento looked about, panic now visible in the old man's eyes. "He is here somewhere. He came through—actually, I had to push him once you jumped—but he did come through."

Sebastian darted away in the direction of the haunted yowl. The wind pushed him from behind and then against him. Cold stabbed through his clothes and he felt the shards on his hands and even on his toes in his boots. The pine branches were unkind to him as he ran springing over logs and feeling the icicle wind against his exposed legs. Sebastian's ankles ached; maybe he twisted them when he came though the painting.

He paused to catch his breath and his shoulders slumped. *When he came through the painting.* Did he really just think that phrase?

The gust spun up loud from behind, like the applause of Caroline's guests at the dinner party, but then died off like his stepmother's silence.

"James!"

Argento trailed ten yards behind, falling further back as the younger man sprinted on. A branch scraped Sebastian's face when he failed to duck in time. There was a blue iridescent glow around him, but it didn't faze him as he ran towards the screaming.

The trees grew thinner as Sebastian plowed through the pines. When he reached the edge of the tree line he saw a figure with bright blonde hair and outstretched arms.

James stood on the edge of a pond. The pines stood in a reverent circle around the crystal waters. The sawing branches grated above, like a crowd of specter woodsmen eager for their craft. The water reflected a mass of silver stars above, each dotted in perfect reflection in the still waters. James' hands were out to the sides, either in questioning or glorious reverence. Even on a closer approach, Sebastian couldn't tell which his friend was feeling. James' gaze rocked up to the sky, then slowly back to the waters, and he groaned again.

He was trembling. He slowly raised one leg as if he were going to kick the glaring spirits of the trees around them, then lurched forward to the water.

"Don't." Sebastian grabbed the back of James' shirt, which was drenched in ice cold sweat, and pulled him back and they both fell to the ground. James' trembling was now a full shake. His eyes were wide and staring up at the freezing, clear sky, and Sebastian saw the dried blood on James' upper lip. There was a dark smudge under James' left eye.

"That water's freezing, man, you'll drown or freeze to death!" Sebastian yelled and covered his friend in his coat. James' skin was frozen and clammy; his teeth chattered.

"No, he won't." Argento was now standing beside them, a satchel in each hand. "That is not water."

"What? You're crazy! Yes it is, it's a pond, look at it." Sebastian pointed out at the still waters.

He caught the blue smudge from the corner of his eye. Sebastian brought his hands back in front of his eyes. They were glowing blue.

"Ahhhh, holy shit!" he screamed, and James joined him, though he was still focused on the sky. Sebastian slapped his blue hands on his coat.

"Stop it!" Argento dropped the satchels on the pine needle carpeting and grabbed Sebastian's glowing hands. "It's the peregrinite."

"How in the hell—" Sebastian struggled against the old man.

"We call it 'the mark of the artist.' It causes our hands to glow." Argento pulled his leather glove off one hand and revealed the same blue glow. "You are not in your world anymore, Sebastian."

The old man turned and took a step into the water. The reflection of the stars above parted around him. Argento continued a few paces more—a pale blue dot hovering where his outstretched hand was—and the reflection rippled like pond water touched by skipping stones, the image swayed like grass. Where there had been smooth glass-like water even in the piercing winds, was a split rippled half-reflection of the night's sky.

"It's a mirror field," Argento called from the center.

"My god," Sebastian muttered.

"It's all wrong!" James screamed. Sebastian jumped, having forgotten his crazed friend sitting next to him. James leaned in close to Sebastian's face and whispered, "They aren't the same." He was pointing up.

Sebastian followed his friend's arm up and looked at the mesmerizing sky. Diamond stars twinkled out of the velvet. The dark cobalt fell away into oblivion in a way only seen in the country, far away from the warm lights of cities and villages. He sighed, enveloped by soft depth and white jewels dusted across the expanse. But where was the big dipper? Where was the Bull or Orion?

James continued to stare at him with his wide, wild eyes.

"Aye, even the skies are different here, gentlemen," Argento had rejoined them on the edge, and the reflecting field had returned to the still, mirror-like appearance as before. "That one is the Earless Man, and that is the Blue Guitar. Oh! And that is Celestine the star-maiden, my granddaughter loved that one…" Argento trailed off, pulling his black glove back on. He spun 'round and walked back to the woods. There was a crunch and Sebastian turned just in time to see James fall forward, sprawled out in the pine needles like a fallen scarecrow.

The thump was louder than Sebastian thought it would be and he leaned over to make sure James' head hadn't landed on a stone. Thankfully it hadn't—James just had a hard head.

The fire glowed in the center of the clearing. Rich smoke twisted up into the dark sky. Now that he was done dragging his unconscious friend back to the clearing, Sebastian plopped to the ground. Argento sat cross legged with his blue hands outstretched over the purple flames.

"So is it the wood or the fire that makes it purple," Sebastian whispered. He knew if he attempted to say what he really thought, that he couldn't give a damn about it, he would most likely send this odd man to the ground.

"The pines of Weldon burn purple in winter, green in summer."

"Amazing," Sebastian mumbled.

Argento glanced at him. "You think I betrayed you, is that

right?” Argento breathed on his cold hands, the blue glow lit up his nose and other features and reflected in his silver hair.

Sebastian said nothing. His confusion was mounting. Although he had been told where they were going, he hadn't believed the old man. It was temporary lunacy mixed with fear, he was sure, that made him jump at his painting.

Sebastian let out a loud sneeze and his reflexes brought his hands to cover his mouth. The world turned to a blue haze.

“Blessings,” Argento said off hand.

“Blessings?” Sebastian shouted. “You call this a blessing?” He waved his hands in Argento's face, the blue motion created a dream-like look.

The old man snatched Sebastian's hand and he flinched.

“Yes I do, Sebastian.” Argento's grip tightened. “I am home. I can try to rescue my granddaughter from a madman. A woman whom I had believed meant something to you, as well.” Sebastian ripped his hands out of the old man's grip and scrambled to his feet. He felt the pressure in his head again for a moment, but it quickly waned.

“Sebastian.” Argento got to his feet. “Why do you set yourself against the winds?”

“What?”

“James and yourself are a funny pair.” Argento chuckled. “You, Mr. Albright, who insists on doing the exact opposite of what people tell you, always set yourself against the winds, even when the winds are blowing you in the correct direction. And James," at the sound of his name, James asked someone to pass the ale and come dance, "he goes with the winds wherever they carry him, for good or folly."

Sebastian looked down at his friend sprawled out near the fire. James was mumbling again and he was pretty sure he said "it's all wrong."

"There are times when the wind blows true, Sebastian." Argento put a hand on his shoulder, the blue visible from the corner of Sebastian's scowling eyes. "You need to learn how to tell when to bend or you will break. Just as James needs to learn when to stand firm or he'll be carried off like fluff from a cattail."

Sebastian jerked his shoulder away, and kicked a log from the fire, sending purple sparks up into the dark sky.

They did not fade away. Sebastian watched the purple sparks float higher. They swirled with the heat into the cold night air, up into the trees like the bright orange and yellow ones at Three Oaks. The winds had dropped to a slow breeze and only the tops of the pines were swaying, barely visible against the deep blue sky.

"It's all wrong…" James muttered again. Sebastian had to agree—they weren't the same stars. But being in another world still wasn't possible.

Maybe they were in Australia—he had heard things were

different there…not people walking upside down like in children's stories, but maybe blue hands or purple flames...

The purple sparks were still floating above his head, but they had been joined by yellow ones—real colors, not imagined memories. These sparks of light left a trail behind them, then changed direction and twisted in on themselves and were joined by more yellows, and a jeweled blue that stood out against the deep eternity of the night's sky. It was no longer sparks but the sky, the stars moving and twisting like they were caught in a night wind.

"How in the…" Sebastian trailed off.

"Ah yes, I've missed seeing the—" Argento began, but Sebastian had already begun running. This time it was in the opposite direction of the mirror field, and he was hit in the face and shoulders by low branches since he kept his face to the sky as he ran. The yellows and jewel-tones grew brighter and more defined, turning and slipping in circles.

Sebastian pushed past the last tree branch and stood on the edge of Weldon Wood.

Only a few meters from the wood's edge was a river, or stream, Sebastian couldn't tell in the strange light. To the east of the stream was a valley of open fields of tall grass. In the distance stood a castle. The bright colors of the swirling sky cast onto the grey stones of the castle, turning it indigo. Sebastian was looking at his painting.

"What do you believe now, Sebastian?" Argento asked in a quiet voice. Sebastian didn't even jump. He just stared out over the scene, his scene, while the stars swirled above.

"Weldon?"

Argento nodded.

A light was glowing in the highest window, the tower. Above the window a flag was stirring in the breeze, one of red, white, and black diamonds.

"Go back to the fire, Sebastian. We won't be saving her tonight."

Chapter 16

She paced the floor, and over these four months back in Weldon she'd worn a circle into her rug, her path to nowhere she referred to it in her mind.

She hated this place. She was only let out of the tower once a week to walk in the kitchen garden for air and to stretch. Knell had called it her weekly stroll, like it was a lovely visit to a cafe or some tea party. Always one of his men walked beside her, inches away so she could feel their hand hovering near her arm, and eyes lingering elsewhere. One time she'd stopped to pick a sprig of mint and the guard backhanded her across the face. She'd returned it with a solid punch to his gut, and ran to the archway exit, hoping to reach a tunnel under Weldon House like she had the year before, only to find Knell standing in the shadows, secretly watching the ordeal for unknown pleasures, she was sure. He yelled at his man to never lay a hand on Lady Weldon again, but had her escorted back to the tower nonetheless.

Knell called himself a caretaker. Less like she was his ward, and more like she was an exhibit in an exotic animal show: one to be admired and kept hidden like a prize.

To an outsider, her cell looked cozy. Rich tapestries hung on the walls, warm blankets and a fireplace to warm her in the cold months. There was a small shelf of white pine next to the locked door packed with several figurines, statues, and trinkets. Each was a gift from her captor. Once she had taken all of them off and hidden them behind the shelf. The next morning they were back in their places, exactly as they had been before.

Months ago she tried to tell herself it was only temporary, this imprisonment. In a short amount of time she will be sitting back on the warm stone on the river, the soft bleating of sheep in the background, the embarrassed laughter of the young artist creating smiles on her face.

Yet, as the dry Autumn had given way to the rains of Winter, and logs began to burn lavender in the grate, she knew she'd had her freedom and lost it. She'd had her chance to prove Grandad was alive and to bring him back to Weldon—and failed.

She gave up her walking and pulled a stool over to the western window and threw the red cushion away across the room, knocking over some new statue left as a token by Knell. She sat at the window watching the cold night approach in the west, laying her bare arms on the sill, not aware, or maybe not caring, that her skin was going numb on the freezing stone.

Anna hadn't slept for a week, and that night sleep caught up with her, fitful and full of shadows. After yet another day of pacing the floors, night began to fall. Once again she went to her window to feel the cold air on her face. As the last edge of the sun slipped behind the peak of Mount Sanzio, Anna sprung to her toes and leaned up against the window frame. She stretched and strained against the trembling roar in her heart, echoing like thunder across Weldon Valley.

Her hands ran in her hair, pulling at the curls until they went flat. Her eyes grew wider as the light slunk away.

Soon there would be the knock, the sad, apologetic knock from Lacy, the girl who made up her room and her one real contact with the outside world in four months. Lacey moved carefully so to keep her bruises covered, but never truly succeeded. Anna didn't blame her for this situation; she was only a girl, no more than fifteen—Knell had taken many prisoners.

"Good evening, miss." Lacey watched the floor as she entered the chamber, right on cue. She did not wear a hat like Anna had during her time at Albright Manor. Her pink frock was covered by a starched white apron, and her auburn hair was twisted into a tight bun at the crown of her head. Lacey's arms were full of new linens for the bed and she scuttled about changing them, but not before locking the door behind her. "Miss, you'll catch a cold with that window open."

Anna sighed. "I will be fine, Lacey, but I thank you for your concern." Anna sighed as the evening star appeared. "When I was almost ten, my Grandad took me for a visit to Castle Belvedere. It is such a marvelous place. Have you been?" Lacey shook her head. "Well, I don't truly think I could describe its uniqueness." Anna leaned back and closed the window. "When I was there, a guardsman told me that rock spirits lived under Mount Sanzio, and that the spirits made peregrinite. Of course, Grandad told me it was just nature's way." She joined Lacey who was making up her bed.

"Do you believe in such things, miss?"

Anna laughed. "I have seen many things, yet a rock spirit is not one of them. I know many things are possible." She smiled only for a moment when the image of a cave painted with figures of animals and courtesans slipped past her memory. "Do you believe it is possible, Lacey?"

Lacey shook her head, her eyes fixated on the sheets. "I dunno, miss."

"You must wonder." Anna prodded.

Lacey flung the fluffy down quilt up in the air and smoothed it out once it floated back in place. "Not much wonder left in this world, I think."

Lacey finished changing the linens and took up the old sheets. Anna went back to her stool by the western window. Just a streak of pale twilight stood against the outline of the Sanzio Mountains, and more stars were beginning to shine. A spark of bright blue drifted across the sky followed by one of yellow. "The star dance is beginning, come watch," Anna called as Lacey was closing the door behind her.

"I can't, miss." The key turned in the lock.

Anna turned out the lamp after sitting at her window for another hour watching the star dance's yellow and blue swirling lights. The room had warmed quickly once the window was closed and sleep came fast this night, a blessing to be sure.

Perhaps that was why she woke with such a start around midnight. She was curled up on her bed against the stone wall, but a low yellow lamplight flickered across, creating shadows and movement. Anna turned over and looked into the low lavender flames in the grate. For a moment the lamp flickered and it looked like a person was sitting in her red armchair.

"Lacey?" she whispered. The lamp turned up.

Victor Knell sat posed on the chair with one leg flung over the arm. In the low light, the black and red tattoos on Knell's face took on a brown color, the white ones glowed bright, making the harlequin pattern seem wrong in some way, as if done incorrectly.

Knell's face hadn't changed much since Anna had been under his care, except for the addition of more patterned marks. Yet in the year since she had left Weldon, escaped to that other place and returned, she noticed his eyes seemed heavier as they stared out from under his thick brows—the only hair on his head.

His tunic bore Knell's signature pattern in a strip down his chest, with matching sleeves. The white background of his tunic glowed like his tattoos.

"Evening, milady."

Anna sat up, and slowly pulled her blanket up around her neck. She was wearing a heavy winter night shirt, but felt exposed nonetheless.

"I'm sorry to have woken you. Usually I try to be very quiet." Knell's voice was gravely and croaking.

Knell had visited her before, but never at night—or at least she never knew he had come in the night. When he visited in daytime he would bring a guard or a servant woman with him. Anna looked around the room and found no others. He also tended to leave a token—a vase of flowers, some little statue. The first time all those years ago when Grandad had disappeared he left a glass bottle filled with sand.

"I heard you find the idea of rock spirits intriguing," Knell continued, as if they had been discussing current events over tea.

Poor Lacey. Anna hoped she hadn't been beaten for that tidbit.

"Yes, it is interesting, to be sure," she answered, pulling the blankets tighter about herself.

Anna reached her hand to her pillow and felt the corner of a parchment. For months she had kept it hidden in her pillowcase. In her mind she saw the sketch Sebastian had given her of Three Oaks. Its yellow tones glowed out from the bonfire into the dark night and the tall oaks overshadowed the scene like the ruins of a sacred temple. In it she was playing the fiddle, the glow of the fire on her face.

"I myself have wondered such things as well," Knell continued, "and the people of Belvedere claim strange things about their mountains, I learned that years ago when traveling out of the Sanzio Mountains on my way to the Dali." Knell smirked.

"Yes, Grandad took me there once."

Knell raised an eyebrow. "I'm positive it was an intriguing experience."

Anna was glancing around her room. On the white pine shelf was a small glass figurine, one she did not recognize. It was a woman dressed in robes. She held a tome in one arm and the other was raised high, holding a torch. The glass had a faint green or teal tint like the glasses Señora Elena used in her tavern in Spain.

"Is that for me?" Anna motioned at the figurine.

Knell smiled. "Of course, milady."

"Thank you," Anna choked.

"You deserve the best. You are after all the Lady of Weldon." Even in the low light, she saw his face curl into a look of arrogance. Anna hated the way he said *Lady of Weldon*. There was something in Knell's tone that made it seem as if she was *his* lady.

She remembered the first time he called her that, she'd been little more than twenty, and Grandad had been missing for three weeks. Knell had approached her in the main hall and knelt on one knee. His face was marked with fewer tattoos than now, but his matching cloak hung on his shoulders as he knelt. She remembered wondering why a circus man was bowing to her, that maybe a servant had sent him to entertain her until Grandad came home.

She shuttered. When the rider who came with Knell that day handed her the parchment, the one with Grandad's letter calling Knell his truest friend, a part of her had wondered if he might truly be dead. Would she have the same fate? Perhaps. There were days when she wondered if Knell would simply throw her into the moat, floating like a water lily, and declare her a crazed lunatic and himself Duke of Weldon. In truth, she wondered why he hadn't already.

Knell was staring at her, posed with an expression Anna could not exactly figure out. Was that confusion, or…

"Are you cold, milady? Shall I send for that girl to stoke the fire?" Knell interrupted her thoughts. He flung his leg off the arm of the chair a bit slower than he had in years past. He looked like he was squatting on the floor, using the chair more as a placeholder.

"Oh no, I am fine…thank you," she answered. The words *Lady of Weldon* whispered in the back of her mind.

Knell leaned back into the high-backed chair, assuming a more relaxed posture. "You have something to say, milady." It was not a question.

While the reputation of Victor Knell's violence and swift revenge was known far, his perceptive nature was not. Anna had learned from the start that very little slipped past the watchful eyes of her tattooed jailer. But there were some things.

"Before, you allowed me free range of Weldon House," Anna said.

"And we both know what you eventually did with that freedom, milady." It was the answer Anna knew he would give, so she hung her head.

"Yes that's true...but I paid the price." She looked at her hands. "Did I ever thank you for saving me, for bringing me home?"

Knell scowled, the black, red, and white pattern wrinkled around his narrow eyes and across his wide forehead.

"Do not lie to me, milady. I do not deal with liars." She heard the razor sharpening in his voice.

"I am not lying," her voice cracked. "The horrors on that side…a man in one city tried to…" She shuttered and the woven blanket slipped off her shoulder. Knell's scowl shifted into a sneer with a twist of anger. Anna knew if that imaginary man had been in Knell's presence he'd be begging for death by now.

"That was why I carried the staff," Anna continued. "After that, seeing Weldon is a relief," she sighed. She felt for the sketch parchment again. "Though I did not appreciate the manner in which I was brought home, I am glad to be here."

Knell grinned, the pattern stretched along his cheeks. "I could not be sure that you would come willingly, so I did what I needed to."

"You mean your henchman did what he needed to?" Anna said with teasing in her voice and a smile playing on her lips.

"Well, someone needed to stay and watch over Weldon for you, Anna." She tried not to cringe when he spoke her name. It was worse than when he said Lady of Weldon. Instead, she nodded.

"I would say that is true." She smiled, hoping the low light would hide her disgust. Her stomach flopped like when the Albright's cook had prepared a dish she called kidney pie.

"But it has been four months since you came home," Knell put a hand to his chin in an overly-postured thinking pose. "I don't think it would be terrible if you were allowed to move about the castle…sometimes."

Anna waited.

"I am not an ungodly man—on Sunday mornings, you could walk the high walls. I believe you liked to walk there as a child?"

"Oh thank you…Victor." She felt her hands tighten under her blanket. "Yes, that would be lovely."

"You are very welcome, milady." He stood, bowed, and turned to leave. "Pleasant dreams."

The key turned in the door.

Chapter 17

Weldon Wood was warmer come the dawn. Even with the overcast skies and patches of fog lending an element of the forbidden or bad luck along with a seeping dampness, Sebastian welcomed it over the piercing wind of the night before. The welcome to this side had not been quite what he had expected.

Yet what he had expected, he wasn't sure. Ponds that were fields, stars and skies that swirled and moved. Blue hands.

Argento had insisted they move on from the area as soon as they had each eaten a few apricots and a fruit they did not recognize that tasted like a cross between blackberry and mint, but looked like a purple apple. "Anything but quince," Sebastian had snickered to James, who smiled but did not laugh.

Only an hour before, James had awoken flailing and screaming about silver, and scalded his left hand in the fire. Argento had cleaned and wrapped it, as well as the cuts on Sebastian's face. Now, James huddled next to the lavender embers of last night's fire. Arms wrapped 'round his knees and rocking slowly, James' wild-eyed look had transformed to a vacant stare.

"What the hell's going on?" James growled, his left eye twitching. Sebastian saw his black eye had darkened and the dried blood was still on his nose—from fainting last night or maybe from when he'd punched him, Sebastian wasn't sure.

"Um, well…"

James clenched his fists and closed his eyes. "I'm hallucinating."

"No, James." Sebastian sat down in the pine needles beside him. He hesitated. Then he blurted out, "Last night we went through my painting because apparently it is a doorway to where Argento is really from."

James kept rocking.

"And he wants us to help him rescue his granddaughter, who is actually Anna from back home."

"Right."

"Oh, and he's a Duke."

James stopped rocking. "So, I've gone mad," he stated.

Sebastian shrugged. "If you have, then I am too." He let out a long breath.

Sebastian chucked a small stone into the fire, but the low fog muffled the crunch of the embers.

"And sorry about your nose and eye, mate."

James touched his nose and flinched. "I think I'll heal, *Master Albright.*" He gave a half-hearted smile. "We went through a painting? How is that even possible?"

Sebastian shrugged. "Damned if I know, but I think it's true. Did you see that sky last night?" James shook his head. "Oh, right. Well how about this—my hands glow blue in the dark!" He raised a gloved hand.

"What?"

"It's true, mate. Scared the hell out of me. Almost collapsed there next to that weird mirror pond like you—but someone had to haul you back to the fire." Sebastian punched James' shoulder.

"Funny."

Sebastian took another purple fruit. "All right, but it is true—Argento's hands did too. He says it's the peregrinite."

"The what?" James asked.

"It's this stuff in his paints, ones he brought from this side."

"Oh, man."

Sebastian nodded.

James let out a long breath and ran a hand through his hair. "And to think I was worried about getting pounded by Porter only a few hours ago." He picked up his satchel and bounced it up and down, feeling the weight. A mischievous smile played on his face. "Wonder if silver is valuable here?"

Sebastian laughed. "I'm guessing it just may be, mate." James joined in the laugher, both men imagining the confusion on Porter's face when his goons tell him they had disappeared.

Argento broke up the laughter by kicking dirt onto the lavender embers.

"We must be off. This way, gentlemen." Argento tapped his brown hat on his head and walked off. He seemed in wonderful spirits, and as they began to walk west through the trees he told James how he had entered their world the first time and how the harlequin-tattooed Victor Knell had taken Anna.

James had no choice but to believe him. How else did he explain this bizarre place with water-fields and the wrong stars, where fires were purple instead of red? Or at least that was what James kept saying in his mind, nodding along as Argento regaled him with his story of a substance that transported him to Italy and made his hands glow blue in the night.

James was warmer now that they were on the move, and thanks to his wool coat. His former master was wearing the blue coat from home. James remembered packing them all those months ago. To think he had been sweltering only hours before.

Duke Weldon, as James was beginning to think of him, looked at a silver compass on his ring and consulted it. The needle pointed north—ah, steady north unlike the slow, maddening circles it spun when he looked on Florence for the first time.

Argento led them through a dense part of the pine forest. When James ducked under the low branches of one tree, to his left saw a yellow glow. Mushrooms of a sort were growing in a moss-covered hollow, though he had never seen ones that glowed in daylight. He took a step closer disturbing the dry leaves underfoot. Eyes turned and stared at James, scanning him from feet to head with curious hunger. James jumped when Argento's hand clamped down on his shoulder and pulled him on.

"It would be wise to move on from there, son." The Duke's tone was like suggesting he order the steak over the fish in a pub. "Ochreites do not take kindly to those who disturb their dens."

"What the hell were those?" James coughed.

Argento paused. "The closest thing I found on your side would be a garden slug." He started walking again but turned around. "If slugs could eat through boots."

James glanced back over his shoulder at the hollow and down at his feet. He shuddered and darted off after his companions.

After a time they skirted the mirror field, but in the daylight it was just another grassy spot with a speckling of winter wildflowers. James quickened his pace as they walked on.

At least the scent was nicer than the rotted fish and stink of seaweed James was almost used to. Chipper birdcall flitted overhead as if the little birds were following the newcomers.

In the dense forest it was difficult to see the sky for long, and though Argento said it was midafternoon, James and Sebastian were feeling lost. Sebastian's forehead was wrinkling into a scowl.

"Where are we going?" James whispered as he pushed past the next prickled branch.

"We are here," Argento called.

It was a small clearing with a crumbled shack in the center. The grey stones that made up the former mill house were covered over in places by ivy and in others by dried out dead mosses. A large tree overhung with moss busted up through the thatched roof, gnarled and wide. A pile of stones laid disjointed on the eastern side, a wall pushed out by the massive roots of the tree.

"Weldon House is looking grand as ever," Sebastian said.

The old man shook his head and ignored him. He side-stepped a pile of thatch that had fallen years ago by the decomposed look of it, and approached the front door of the shack at a creep. Argento pulled off his velveteen hat and bent over, searching the doorframe. "Ah. Yes, this is it." He stood upright, replaced his hat, and pushed the wooden door open.

James followed after the Duke, but Sebastian paused at the door. It took a moment for his eyes to adjust to the dimness once inside the dilapidated shack. James was poking around an over-turned cupboard, tossing empty tins and half-spent candles aside, and Argento was nowhere to be seen. The floor was littered with droppings and broken dishes. Sebastian walked around the thick, gnarled tree trunk. It was almost like an oak tree, but not a variety he recognized. The sprawling branches were void of leaves, but still had the remnants of many bird's nests. The branches pushed through the roof, dislodging thatch and letting in a filtered sunlight that speckled the floor, which had at one time been wood, but was now tamped dirt.

"Lovely, almost as nice as the boarding house," Sebastian

quipped.

"Come on, a bit further," Argento called. The two younger men filed out of the tree room and into a back washroom of sorts with a small sink toppled to the floor. A back door stood open only because it was hanging by the bottom hinge alone. They ducked under the jutting door, back into the foggy morning.

Argento had dropped his satchel into the scrub grass that was growing a few feet tall and had one foot up on a moderately large boulder. Pine needles and leaves had been pushed aside along the dirt in front and a fresh piece of the rock stood out in contrast to the grimy moss-covered section above.

"If you don't mind, gentlemen." Argento pointed at the rock. "I thought I could move it, but alas I'm older than I was when I left, you know."

James looked at Sebastian as if this was the craziest thing yet, and Sebastian seemed to agree.

"You want us to move this boulder?" James asked.

"Why yes, my good man."

Sebastian scratched his head and shrugged. "Fine."

The three of them leaned against the boulder. After about ten seconds of pushing James heard a click and a slice of the rock slid across and away. Sebastian lost his balance and fell, knocking James to the ground.

"I see some things are the same here as in your land!"

Argento laughed. Sebastian scowled as they got to their feet and dusted off the pine needles.

The hole was black inside and all that could be seen was the top of a rope ladder. A smell of must and old vegetables seeped out.

Argento was humming a tune and placing his hat in his bag. He swung it out and down the hole. A soft thud echoed back showing that the hole wasn't deep, even if the ladder gave way, which it looked likely to do, it wouldn't be too hard a fall. But getting back out was another thing.

In the same manner as how they had entered the tree-filled house, Argento took the lead. He tested the upper rung, and once he was satisfied, started to climb down.

"Come on lads!" he yelled up.

"What do you think?" James asked Sebastian.

"I think he's mad." Sebastian squinted down the hole.

"Well, you make-up your mind up here."

"You're going down there?"

"Sebastian, I woke up this morning on the other side of a painting. Climbing down a hole is nothing!" James dropped down and Sebastian heard the thud of his feet hitting the ground.

He stood on the edge. He couldn't see either Argento or James, but he thought he heard them whispering.

"Are you setting yourself against the wind again?" Argento's frustrating voice called from the blackness.

"It wasn't very windy up there, more foggy," he heard James remark.

"Oh for the love…" Sebastian started, but he pitched his satchel into the hole then flung his leg over the side and climbed down.

It was pitch black as expected. The smell of vegetables was much stronger, though it also reminded him of river sand, like his cave by the willow.

"James? Argento?" he called.

"Um, this way, I think," James answered. Sebastian turned and saw a pale blue glow from a bit off.

"Now would be a good time to take off your gloves," Argento called and waved his glowing hands about. The glow left trails of soft light as he moved his hands.

Sebastian did as suggested.

"Good lord!" James exclaimed.

The blue glow of Sebastian's hands worked like a lantern of sorts and he could see they were in a tunnel. Along the walls were graffiti-like carvings decorating the length. He put a hand against the jagged wall and felt the carvings—names, dates, words he couldn't read and images of people in circumstances he didn't understand. He remembered his cave by the willow back home and thought how beautiful some of his drawings would have looked in a blue light. He inched along the walls, feeling and seeing the images and words at once. He paused as his fingers traced the initials A.L.

"Anna," he whispered. He moved his hand along the carving and read her message: "I go in search of DW. I will never believe he is dead!"

Then below her declarative statement read another: "I'll not let the Knell ring for Me."

Argento was moving off down the tunnel still humming his tune with James close behind, when Sebastian realized he'd heard the tune before—in his own cave next to the river when Anna had helped him finish a painting of some waves on a shoreline. "They crash on angles, breaking on the rocks, I remember it. You capture it well." She'd smiled up at him while she had crouched close to the wall.

Sebastian shuttered and ran off to catch up with Argento and James.

"She left her name back there—Anna!" Sebastian panted when he caught up with them. "She was here!"

"I saw." Argento kept moving. "I showed her these tunnels years ago. Apparently she used them to escape Knell the first time."

Sebastian ran his blue hand through his hair. "You never told us how she escaped him before. Do you even know?"

Argento stopped. His hair reflected his blue hands, making him look as if he were struck by blue lightning. "I do not know for certain. When I spoke with her in Spain, I could not let her know my identity, it was too risky. This meant I could not ask her about Weldon or Knell." James clapped his shoulder. "I kept my face hidden from her, I said I was disfigured and showed no one my face." Argento faltered, the last word caught in his throat. "She gave me directions to a safe house, so I could get food and clothes if I needed it."

Sebastian looked away, remembering her story of living with the nuns in Spain, how they'd taken her in and mended her foot. He envisioned Anna telling the masked Argento of the friars of San Judas Tadeo. He felt the wooden coin in his pocket.

Argento wiped his eyes, "Yet, knowing my granddaughter, I believe she most likely escaped Weldon through the catacombs. Weldon is a land of many springs and each springtime they flood. They would have been a perfect way to escape Knell, should he have used dogs or other trackers…"

Sebastian leaned against the cavern wall. How much longer would it be until she might try again, he wondered, and would she even get a chance with Knell this time?

"If they flood in spring, then they may still be empty now," James offered.

"By now there would be the beginnings, but even so, she would have to reach the high walls first, I'd gather," Argento replied. "From the highest walls there is a hidden staircase leading down our main well. It is accessed in the catacomb entrance, by our kitchens.

I know she used to go that way some days to evade her teachers."

Sebastian laughed and punched James on the shoulder. "Sound familiar?"

Argento walked on again, leading them further away from Anna's message.

It was hot in the tunnels—Sebastian assumed it would be cold, but he was back to roasting like in Port City.

"Why is it so blazing hot down here?" he grumbled while peeling off the coat Argento had packed from home. Ahead of him James stumbled and swayed and he trailed his right hand against the tunnel wall.

"Thermal vents from Mt. Sanzio," Argento answered. Sebastian saw the old man run his blue hands through his silvery hair. He was suffering too. "Only a bit farther, I believe." It was difficult to say how far they had walked in such complete darkness.

But the hours passed. Onward they trudged, led by the blue haze from his and Argento's hands. The blue glow from the peregrinite only illuminated a few feet in front of him, and his companions were more like shadows or outlines depending on how his arms swung.

For a while James had kept track of the turns—left, right, left, left, right—but he'd given up after his fifth stumble. The tunnel floor was clear for the most part but there was a stray stone here and there seeking feet to trip. Argento explained that most of these tunnels were old mining shafts and had been abandoned decades before he took over Weldon.

The smell changed as they moved further into the tunnel. The rotted plant scent was replaced with a gritty mineral scent. Every few steps there was a hint of sulfur. Sebastian had visions of turning a bend and coming face to face with Satan—if they moved any further down, who knows. He assumed the Devil existed on this side of paintings—evil certainly did. Or perhaps the Dark One had already taken up residence at Weldon House.

Sweat poured down Sebastian's face. Going from extreme heat in Port City to the frigid night cold in the woods to this was wreaking havoc. His muscles were cramping, and he shivered but felt the sweat drip down his forehead and onto his lashes. He raised his blue hand to his face and whipped away the drops, pausing to steady the shaking.

Moving the bright glow so close to his eyes made him squint, and through the slits he saw the white glow of James' blond hair to his left. James must have stopped or maybe he'd caught up with him, Sebastian thought.

"Hey, you all right, mate?" Sebastian muttered across his left shoulder.

"What?" James called from five yards ahead of him. Sebastian dropped his glowing hand and twisted up in the voice's direction. There was the outline of James through Argento's blue glow. When Sebastian flicked back to the left the white glow came into focus as a white featureless face.

"Son of a bitch!" Sebastian yelled and stumbled to Argento and James.

The face floated after him.

"Sweet Lord, what the hell?" James yelled.

"Get back!" Sebastian yelled and swung his fist out at the face in a blue haze, but missed by feet as it dodged to the side.

Argento sprinted in front of the two younger men who were now flattened against the tunnel wall.

The white face crept closer to them and was soon joined by a dozen more—each floating in the air, the pale white surrounding dark sockets but no eyes.

"Run!" Sebastian pushed James but behind them was another group of ethereal faces, silent oval shapes so white the glow was blinding in the tunnel's darkness.

"Halt!" a face near Argento yelled. "Ye are tresspassin' on the Lands of Belvedere!"

James felt a sharp jab in his back and spun around. "The face has a sword!" James yelled.

"How's that possible?" Sebastian yelled back. "It's a face!"

"Silence!" the face said. Its voice echoed down the tunnel.

The faces floated back as one glided forward to them. "Where'd ye get the blue hands—thief?"

"This man is an artist, my good man," the Duke stated.

Laughter echoed through the tunnel.

"Of course, what were we thinking? Artists! Empty your pockets," the lead face demanded. Each of them was poked in the back again.

"I demand to see the Lady!" Argento stated. He said it plainly, as if he were ordering a meal in a tavern.

Cold whispers ran through the floating faces as they turned to each other.

"The Lady does not take demands. Not from thieves such as you," the lead face growled low. Sebastian raised his fist but stealth was not an option as the blue glow reflected on the white faces.

"Think not of it, thief!" a face next to him said.

"No, Sebastian," Argento echoed the face's warning. He lowered his hand but kept the fist tight.

"Now, I repeat, take us to see the Lady. I know of your laws, and it is written that I have a right to face her." Argento's voice was cool.

The faces whispered again.

"Silence!" the lead face shouted. "He speaks true. We will take you thieves to see the Lady."

Argento nodded.

A sword poked them each again until they started marching after the first group of faces back in the direction they had come.

Sebastian put his blue hand out in front of him and could see a black shirt and breeches of a man in front of him. He also could see the scabbard at his side. The men were wearing white masks.

"You're a man?" Sebastian stopped and questioned, then stumbled forward again as he was jabbed in the back.

"A'course I am! You think I'm a troll?" the face laughed and was joined by the others.

"Nah, I'm a frog," another offered.

"Aye yer wife thinks so, Lucas!"

"But not me mistress!" The voices came from all around, each face bobbing a bit with laughter.

"These are Belvedere guards," Argento leaned over and whispered to Sebastian behind a blue hand, "and now it appears we are their prisoners." The last bit was said with the slightest of smiles.

"Wonderful," James mumbled.

They trudged along stumbling in the pale blue of Sebastian and Argento's hands, and the lone lavender torch a guard had lit up ahead.

Chapter 18

The walls towered over them. When he and Sebastian had first wandered the streets of Port City, he'd thought no city or wall could be so high. Of course, those buildings were straight and these city walls were…not. James leaned back to take in the height but saw the way each wall twisted back—as if the beams connecting the aqueducts crisscrossing the city were both sloping down to the main street and flowing away. James tottered, and with his hands bound by the guards he couldn't keep his pace. A guard steadied him but also shoved him in the back with the butt of his sword as they marched past the citizens of the strange city Argento had called Belvedere.

They'd walked for miles through the tunnels, guards marching them faster when it pleased them. Sebastian and Argento were called "thief" at each mention; James was called nothing. After the hours of hot tunnels, reaching the surface again was more than a relief. It was a moment of normalcy and dawn light—until they were spun around to face the main gates of Belvedere. It felt to James that they were walking towards the gates, and away at the same time.

"Keep walking," the guard sneered. A blacksmith they passed eyed the group through squinted eyes, as did a group of elderly women.

"Sebastian," James whispered. "What the hell is wrong with

this place?"

Sebastian turned slowly to look back at him. "Where do you want me to begin?"

"Look at their water culverts! How is it possible for—how can it flow two ways at once?"

Sebastian shrugged. James saw how much his former master was starting to resemble Argento.

The guards, who now wore the white masks around their necks like pendants, marched them down the main thoroughfare. The road was paved with black sandstones—golden rocks punctuated the spaces between the stones. Much the same was true of the low walls lining each side of the street. Dark, heavy stones hewn in perfect rectangles from the same sandstone as the street. Every few feet a golden pebble was sunk into the black mortar creating a hypnotizing repetitive pattern.

The road was leading to a large castle. Castle Belvedere stood high on the hill, nestled between the crags of the Sanzio Mountains, black rocks rising above the highest towers of the castle. Turrets poked into the sky, black flags whipped in the winds from a massive waterfall coursing behind the main castle. To the sides, smaller offshoots perched on other rocky outcroppings with long ornate bridges connecting them to the main building. James guessed the spray from the waterfall would make the walkways slick, like the docks in a stormy sea.

Once the group had marched through the portcullis, a guard poked Sebastian in the back, ushering them to the right of the main gate. Around the side was another door, one hardly noticeable and very likely designed for castle servants. They were shuffled through the door and into a small courtyard and potager garden.

"There's nothing quite as satisfying as the joy of seeing an old friend, especially one who is dead." The woman kept her gaze on the woven basket resting on her lap. She sat on a cement bench just on the dark side of a shade line. All around her bench grew rosemary—the pungent scent hung around them, a glimpse of bright summer in frigid winter. The woman's clothes were black silks with the faintest golden embroidered lines. She wore a thin black veil on her head that trailed down over her black hair, which she wore loose but pulled behind her ears.

She glanced up at them, and on her lips played the slightest of smiles—she knew something but was keeping the knowledge hidden—at least for the moment.

Sebastian looked around. The small garden was woven with golden rock pathways and heaps of woody herbs mixed with the splashes of rosemary near the woman's bench. A tall lemon verbena stretched on the cloister's northern wall, which was plastered in a warm, golden earth tone. Along a wall with an arched doorway ran a fountain of sorts, the water flowed down into another trough yet moved upwards from the landing point.

The sun shone down bright from above, though their breath hung in front of them. James quaked forward, bumping into Sebastian who grimaced and pushed him back, almost knocking over a delicate topiary on a grey pedestal.

"Lady Gioconda, here are the three thieves we found in the tunnels." The guard bowed.

"Thank you, Maurice. Take the younger two to the catacombs, but leave the grey-haired impersonator."

Before the guard could bow in agreement, Argento pulled free.

"You know the truth! I see it in your eyes. That coy smile does not fool me."

James was shocked at the boldness of the old man, and Sebastian looked at his mentor with astonishment and surprise.

"You know me," Argento continued on. He'd taken a few steps closer and the Lady only needed to glance to tell her guard not to stab this old man where he stood.

"I knew the Duke of Weldon. He was murdered. A jester in colored clothing now sits as Weldon's Regent. My old friend is gone." The Lady spoke in a cool tone, a music of steadiness fell from her lips. The ending of her smooth song toyed with the idea of a question, but only to a skilled ear.

Argento shook his head.

"True, a madman walks Weldon House. And true, he tried to

kill me but instead sent me wandering," his voice held for a moment on the word, and the Lady turned her glance slightly more to face him. "I spent time in a far off land. One of strange ways and no paths home. Until I met these gentlemen."

She took a paused look at the two younger men. She recognized them for what they were: headstrong, confused, determined, a thief and a joker, and obviously not from Belvedere—possibly this realm.

James looked away from her steady stare and bowed his head to her. Sebastian gave a slight nod, but watched his mentor. Her mouth turned that slight smile at his loyalty to his teacher.

"He bears the mark." A gruff guard pulled Sebastian's arm up and removed his glove. Sebastian yanked free and scowled.

Lady Gioconda raised an eyebrow. "Show me." Argento nodded so Sebastian put out his hand, unhappily. Even in the brightness of the courtyard, the faint blue was shimmering.

"He's a thief!" Another guard sneered.

"Go to hell," Sebastian told the guard. One of the men kicked the back of his leg and he fell to the ground. Sebastian whirled around, blue fist raised.

"Stop."

Lady Gioconda rose from her bench and came over to Sebastian. She put out her hand and Sebastian showed her his again.

"This is the mark of the artist. It is too pronounced for a thief or even a miner." She turned to Argento. "You speak true."

"Yes, my old friend."

"Duke Weldon." She opened her arms and embraced him. "It is more than a joy to know you are alive. And I must hear your story. Wanderers are rare." She took Argento by the arm and began to walk to the castle door.

"But I must tell you, Knell has Annalisa."

The Lady froze. "I know."

Argento looked confused. "Then why haven't you–"

Lady Gioconda turned towards the castle entry. "Take these trespassers away, but the Duke must come with me."

"Wait! You just said we weren't thieves!'' Sebastian yelled.

"Again, that is true." She put a hand to Sebastian's cheek. "You are a trespasser in the lands of Belvedere." She made a sharp nod to the guard and Sebastian didn't have a chance to argue as a guard grabbed his arm. He just caught a slip of Argento's face as he and James were swept away through the arched doorway and out of the little garden courtyard. Argento looked as shocked as he was.

~~~~~

Moss hung down from the damp, curved brick ceiling of the tunnel, the sand floor leading to a spacious wine cellar. Various sized crates filled with bottles of wine and other tributes from the lands he ruled lined the edge of the tunnel and the small room where tallow
~~~~~

candles burned yellow light across the space. In the center was a small table where Knell sat.

Simon sat halfway on one of the crates marked pinot grigio, his white mask on the crate beside him, and black cape slung over the chair opposite the one his employer occupied.

He had ridden all night. Once he had been dismissed from his guard duties for the day, he had marched to the halfway house and inn he called home and hired a horse from a bar patron, one only too happy to offer once his finger was broken.

Knell sat jovially at the small table—a glass of strong, deep red was almost empty, and the dinner of pheasant and spring beans happily consumed.

Simon waited for his master to speak first. He had learned after many years in his employ that speaking before the changeable man was usually how men ended up as bones fading to dust in Terry's Flat.

Knell threw his napkin on the table and downed the rest of his wine.

"Make your report quick, my Captain. There's a duty I must perform in my chambers," Knell snickered.

"Of course, my lord." Simon stood up. He cleared his throat. "The Duke of Weldon has returned." Simon stared into his master's eyes—narrow and easy to miss in the patterned tattoos of his face.

Knell twitched—not just his eye or leg—his whole body

made one slight, jagged jolt. The drips of wine still in his glass sloshed.

"How do you know this, my good man?" Simon could hear Knell's teeth grind.

"My lord, I was part of the patrol squad that brought him to Lady Gioconda herself. He and two other men were found in the peregrinite caves. The squad commander arrested him and they were led to the castle to meet her. After that I was dismissed and came here."

In the silence that followed, Knell was very still—the only notion that he hadn't died sitting in his jaunty pose in his chair was the intermittent flicker of the candle as he let out long breaths.

"Well, this is truly fascinating news, my good man. Truly fascinating…" he trailed off. "How could the good Duke have found a way back I wonder…and with collaborators, it seems…"

"We used the traveling device to bring Lady Weldon back." Simon immediately regretted saying anything about this as Knell's eyes flashed at him. Simon had no problem making them out this time.

"Yes, Simon." Knell stretched, swiveling his weight to the other side and dropping the left leg over the arm of his chair.

"I am supposed to report for duty with my patrol squad at dawn. I will be missed for certain." Simon picked up his white mask. From his spot in the dim shadows the mask glowed—yet not as well as it had in the caves.

Knell was rubbing his face—the pattern of black, red, and white diamonds shifted as he pressed his skin. Like Simon's mask, the white diamonds gave off an iridescent glow.

"Well, if you will be missed, then you must depart." Knell swept a hand across in a large gesture motioning to the dark sand-floored tunnel.

There had been many times Simon had assisted Knell in his exploits, even helped acquire the traveling device for him from a hermit of Terry's Flat, and he was quite aware of the physical agility of his master. Years had passed, yet Knell still was capable of springing forth like a viper.

Simon spent his youth on the streets of Belvedere. Even now, he knew the best places to hide from the guards, and where the waterways switched directions. As the son of a peregrinite miner, he had little else to do. He learned to fight—and how to see the weakness in a person. He may not have spent his days in school rooms, but Simon's education was thorough.

When he'd reached the age of decision, his father begged him to join the other miners and him down in the belly of the dark mountains. But instead he spent his nights in pubs—antagonizing the Belvedere guardsmen and spending his days in jail.

Until one morning. He had just been let go by the guard with a warning that one more time and he'd hang, for all the trouble he was worth. As Simon passed by a boarded up theatre a hand grabbed him from behind, covering his mouth, and another hand held a blade to his back. He was pushed into an alley where a covered cherry-colored cart sat.

"Up you go, my good man," a voice said in his ear, so up he went into the wagon.

It was there that Simon met his future employer. But he was given a choice: work for Victor Knell, a strange and energetic man with a face covered in a harlequin pattern; or be hung by the guardsmen in the next week for certain. The brash Simon, son of a miner, asked Knell why he'd mutilated his own face. Knell answered him and pointed to the spot where the next diamond would go when he killed Simon himself.

"It'll be a red one this time."

When Simon looked back at his master, still sitting with one leg slung over the arm of his chair, he saw Knell's left index finger tapping his face—a spot without a diamond.

"My lord, do you have instructions for when I return to Belvedere?" Simon asked.

Knell slipped his leg down and leaned into the candlelight.

"Sit down, Captain."

Chapter 19

She woke early to Lacey rapping at her door, so apologetic as usual. Anna dressed in her boots, as suggested by her lady's maid, and followed her to the kitchens and through the galley passages—ones she'd loved taking with Grandad when they would go exploring in the woods or fields—then they met her captor at the lower exit.

He stood high, tall and puffed, straining to be still and gallant. He wore his signature cape turning him into a harlequin colored stain on the crisp golden morning. His tattoos ever-shocking no matter how many times she saw them, how many years or how the number had grown.

Knell flung his cape and offered her his arm. She took it with manufactured kindness. As they strode away, Lacey scurried back into Weldon House.

Knell led her through the field and down to the river. The river tumbled along its path, the same today as yesterday. Rocks became smooth, dunked in the flow. Water spun in shallows, and paused in rushes where swans sat in safety. Dark blues, tumbling along.

Sebastian had painted the river with a deep blue like this, adding the willow and the hint of the cave in one of his smaller paintings. Anna smiled.

"You enjoy the river, do you not, Lady Weldon?" Knell

spoke, breaking her musings on her artist. She nodded in agreement and kept on strolling. *Sebastian wouldn't believe any of this*, she thought. His mouth would have dropped open like a fish had she told him about Knell. And she paused, realizing again that it was impossible to see him again. "Another realm," she whispered.

"What was that?" She heard the bit of loathing in Knell's voice.

"Slippery stones," she said louder to him, and stepped slowly over the many river rocks, careful not to stumble.

Knell nodded. Why couldn't she have just walked the high walls as he'd promised? Hearing this river, smelling the silty earth instead of watching the sunrise and feeling a breeze in her hair on the high wall, the elemental scent of Weldon, that throughout her travels she had not smelled in any locale. She could have confirmed that her escape passage was still unfound. The edge of rebellion was itching her skin again. She'd known freedom and still had a mission; playing the prisoner would stand no longer.

Her foot stepped over a small pile of stones and into a soft bit of river sand.

It reminded her of when she had bumped over a blue-grey vase he'd given her, which slipped to the floor, spilling out sand. At the time Anna's first reaction was thankfulness that the vase hadn't shattered, though a long crack slipped up to the rim. She'd knelt on her floor and scooped the sparkling sand a handful at a time back into the vase when her hand gripped something small and metallic. She let the sand slip through her fingers till only a small cufflink remained in her palm.

It had the symbol of a winged ox—Grandad's cufflink.

Many believed the Duke of Weldon was dead, and this cufflink would have been the proof. But to Anna—something in her changed. She felt an odd calm and heat in her chest like a spark of fire.

That same night, as was the ritual of Weldon, Anna had joined Knell in the great dining hall. Arriving early, she'd set the vase at Knell's spot.

She sat in her chair, looking at the blues, greens, and yellows shining down across the room from the ceiling's stained glass window. The scene of a ground spring and lush meadows shone down on her.

"Good evening, Anna!" Knell had bellowed as he strode into the room. In his normal fashion, he sprung into his chair keeping his eyes on her, more acrobatic than gentlemanly, and reached for his wine glass. His outstretched hand grasped the vase. Startled, only for a moment, Knell swung it over towards her.

"I believe that this is yours, my young ward. Did you misplace it perhaps?" he had chuckled and slid the vase full of sand across the table to her.

"No, I did not."

Knell paused again, this time with his wine glass properly in hand, and frowned. "You no longer care for my gift? Now what could have changed your mind such?"

Anna did not answer him, but instead pushed back her chair and rose slowly. She picked up the blue-grey vase, more of a bottle than a true vase as she now examined it, and tilted it over.

Grains of sparkling cream colored sand spilled out and spread quickly on the dining hall floor, scattering on the red tile. As the last bit drained from the opening, Anna raised the bottle high and smashed it on the tile floor at Knell's feet.

He jumped up and away from the shards. A metallic clink echoed against the stone as an onyx circle dropped and bounced and sputtered across the tiles, coming to a stop at Knell's boot-tip.

"I believe you know what that is, do you not?" Anna's voice was low but still carried across the grand room.

He plucked up the circle and flipped it into the air like a coin. He caught it with his left hand and opened his palm. Reflecting in the golden light of the stained glass ceiling was the cufflink, the imprint of the ox glinting in the light.

"Isn't this fancy?" Knell laughed. "Didn't your grandfather wear something like this?" He held up the cufflink.

"What did you do with him?" Anna growled. The hairs on the back of her neck stood and her hand clenched the back of her chair, the soft yellow velvet cushion was pressed into the hardwood underneath. She knew if she let go she'd leap out and strangle him. She also knew he'd kill her.

"Why, nothing. The late Duke Weldon was a true friend, and other than watch over you and watch over Weldon like any good ruler—"

"You are not the ruler of Weldon!" Anna yelled.

Knell's wide smile melted down to a thin line. The raised outline of his first tattoo twitched under his eye.

"I am Annalisa Lenore, Lady of Weldon, and *if* my grandfather is truly in the afterlife, then *I* am the ruler of Weldon." Anna's voice had gone quiet but it echoed across the room like a ripple in the water. "You are no longer needed here."

She saw him twitch, a full body spasm. He began to lift his hand up to his patchwork of diamonds on his face, hesitating in a vacant spot.

"You will be gone by dawn," Anna stated.

Knell looked more like a viper than ever. He made only a slight bow and slithered from the dining room.

That was the night she ran. There was no chance of Knell obeying her wishes, but his anger and shock was all she needed to slip up to the highwall walk, down her passageway to the kitchen tunnels, and across the river to find Grandad. By dawn, she was into the peregrinite tunnels.

Even standing near the roar of the rushing waters of the river, she heard the sound of the cufflink on the tiled floor. Her hands clenched tight.

"I thought that perhaps seeing the river in all its glory would remind you, milady, of how small you are. But I sense that I may have been mistaken." Victor Knell rose from his squatting position at the water's edge and swirled about to face the Lady of Weldon standing over him with a smooth grey river rock raised high above her head. She'd missed her moment, and she knew it.

Knell lunged, grabbing her wrist in a strangling grip. The rock shuttered in her hand and she faltered. Adrenaline pumped through her and she shook. Knell's eyes grew wide and his eerie smile spread across his face, distorting the tattoos, stretching the colors. It was like she could see his blood pumping through those red diamond patches—faster right as he lunged, but slower and more calm as his grip on her right wrist grew tighter. Her fingers were growing numb—she then realized his other hand was pinning her left arm against her own waist. Then she felt his fingers lightly stroking her back while he held down her arm.

There it was: the question she'd long considered finally answered. He desired her. It would have been simplest to take as his own the heir of Weldon and secure his place as the ruler of this region. She'd wondered since his arrival why she'd never been given more than a polite glance, or the stern back hand when her questions displeased him. Perhaps not being of the age of decision had stopped him. Or perhaps, why bother when there were many other nameless serving women to comfort him?

"Oh Lady Weldon, if only you had consented. Oh if only." Knell took in a sharp breath by her ear. "You know firsthand what I do to those who upset my wishes. You know how I repay those who betray me. And I had decided to give you another chance. I brought you back to your home, even after you'd escaped. Your small, delusional hope that your beloved grandfather was still alive, when we both know exactly what I did to him. And now, my Lady Weldon, you will suffer the same fate as he, but oh, I think I shall find a much more entertaining way to execute this plan."

Anna's eyes turned dark.

"Does this seem small to you?" she whispered and twisted her right wrist free of his grip, smashing the stone into his face. As it slammed against Knell's left temple his head flung back and his grip on her left wrist loosened. She kicked out at his knee and stumbled to the damp grass.

Anna jolted back to her feet, ignoring the pulsing pain in her foot of her old injury flaring hot, and ran upstream. In half a mile was an old crossing, and that's all she needed: find the crossing and get back to the woods. Lose the madman in those woods. Her heart beat fast and she ran hard, seeing the wooden bridge grow larger up ahead, touched with fog on the edges like it was floating above the fast moving waters. If only the river wasn't frigid, or as fast, or full of jagged rocks then she could have—

Anna crashed to the mucky ground and slid a few feet, covering her dress in a layer of muck.

"Oh, Lady Anna," Knell huffed out, breath ragged and face dripping a red much brighter than his tattoos. He knelt down in the muddy grasses and put his arm hard against her neck, pinning her to the ground. "I admit your daring is impressive for a high class woman, though your family tree boasts at least one other daring member, so perhaps I should not be surprised. Yet, we both know what happened to him when he disobeyed my wishes, do we not, milady?" he repeated. Knell's face sunk in, hanging inches from hers.

"The Duke of Weldon lives. I'll never believe otherwise." Anna shuttered. The involuntary spasm seemed to please him, prove he controlled her.

"Believe what you wish, I care not any longer." Knell sneered. "For a time I believed it necessary to keep an heir to your line alive in Weldon, but now I do not." Anna struggled under his weight. "Stop moving!" He slapped her hard across the face and she felt blood in her nostrils as her face hit the mud. He dragged his hand under her nose to wipe her blood. She snorted and he grinned in satisfaction.

Knell sprung up, and jerked Anna to her feet—she felt the heat in her foot and the throbbing in her nose. He spun her around, standing behind her and forced her hands together.

As he tied her fists together he spoke, his voice much changed, even musical. "Well this just won't do, will it? A lady should never be so unkempt. I'll have that serving girl help you clean up. The former Lady of Weldon should be dressed properly for a trip."

Knell pushed her up the embankment. Anna saw the wooden crossing out the corner of her eye. The fog was lifting.

Chapter 20

It wasn't the worst jail, to be sure. It was clean and warm, with two beds stacked atop each other along one wall. The place was dark, except for an oil lamp burning yellow on a rickety wooden table with only three legs. It wasn't like a bar stool, balanced, but instead missing one leg at a corner. Like the multitude of waterways crisscrossing the city, it boggled James' mind how it could physically stand on three legs. It seemed that much of Belvedere should be leaning or falling, yet it stood strong in its strangeness.

Compared to the small cells of the Port City constabulary, this was like a fancy inn saved for traveling silk merchants. The lack of drunken cellmates was pleasant. Sebastian and James had slept in worse places. One night on their trek to Port City, they'd had to share an attic with a group of five brutes who'd not seen wash water in years and reeked of soured beer and onions.

"So we get private accommodations?" Sebastian had asked the Belvedere guardsman who confiscated his gloves then shoved them into their cell. "When is supper? I'd prefer steak, but I'll take lamb chops, but no mutton. And can you bring us some of your best wine? Something red will do nicely!" He continued to yell out the bars as the guard marched away.

James plopped to the lower bed.

"I'd watch for fleas—not sure they've changed the linens

since the last prisoners," Sebastian muttered and sat on the ground.

"Maybe you should have asked for that with your wine…sir."

He glared at James.

Sebastian ran his hands through his hair—he couldn't remember the last time he'd bathed. He laughed. If only Caroline could see him—he'd love to watch her dainty frame squirm as he entered one of her dinner parties, covered in dirt and grit, smelling of sweat and damp and sea water. Her eyes would go wide with shock—then grow small to slits of hysterical anger.

The hours passed slowly, the only thing drowning out Sebastian's rage was the waterfall. Through the half-circle window at the top of one wall, across a wide square full of passing people, of which only boots and hemlines were visible to them, was a monumental waterfall. Beginning in the deep caverns of the mountains, it cascaded down six hundred feet, spraying a turquoise mist up, filling the square like fog.

The bottom of the falls couldn't be seen, but the echo made it known to be hundreds of feet below the edges of Belvedere, flowing into the river, down through the woods and on to Weldon.

The low fog filled the square, clinging to the black stones in soft clumps. They shifted by the windows, slipping along crevasses, leaving an odor of effervescent minerals in their wake.

"Wonder why they give prisoners so nice a view?" Sebastian

snorted. James stood at their cell doors, head hung against the wrought iron, hands hanging through the bars. There was a yellow glow out in the corridor, a low golden glow of life, like sun in spring. But with the black stones that made up the walls, it turned dingy, apart from the flecks of gold now and then that twinkled from the stone.

The hallway must have been linked to an airshaft, James thought as he leaned against the bars. At least the air seemed a bit fresher. It could be in his head, but after three days, he didn't care. Anything to not smell the dank grit of the drips from the window Sebastian refused to move out from under. The fool.

"Hey! Why are we in here?" Sebastian jumped up and charged the cell bars. "What'd you do with our friend? The old man?" He shook the bars.

"Sebastian, stop!"

Sebastian swung around and upended the three-legged table. The crash echoed in their cell.

"Well, that's wonderful." James shook his head.

Sebastian ignored him and kicked at one of the legs—the mystery of how it stood on only three legs never to be known—until it snapped off. He picked up the oil lamp, thankfully still lit he thought, and stuck in one end of the leg.

"What are you—" James began.

"I'm getting us outta here—I'm setting myself against the

wind and I don't care!" He ranted.

James stood back, leaning against the bars of their cell. He'd seen Sebastian like this before, when an inspiration took hold and he'd spend all day in his workshop. Each time an amazing painting would emerge. He learned long ago not to interfere with the inspiration—though it was more like madness.

For almost two hours Sebastian moved with determination, guiding the charred end of the table leg on the plastered wall of their cell. After a time, James saw the image coalesce into a wood, there was a cottage and a stream—the peasant version of Weldon House.

When the stick dropped to the floor, James jumped off the bed.

"What do you think?" Sebastian whispered. He was standing back from the wall, surveying the image.

The stream looked like it was moving along, a small paddle wheel gliding in circles. There was even the faintest smell of wood smoke like the puffing chimney of the small thatched-roof cottage.

"God," James muttered. "It's wonderful."

Sebastian seemed far away—was he looking into the far away woods? He was taking deep, slow breaths. He clenched his fists, the blue glow intensified ever so briefly, and let out a primal yell. Sebastian charged at the image, shoulder down like jumping through a glass window, and bounced off the plaster.

His primal yell morphed into a groan of agony as he clenched his shoulder and stumbled to the floor.

James jumped up and helped him to lean up against his drawing.

"There must be some kind of way outta here!" Sebastian shuttered—rage or fear—James couldn't tell.

"Damn it! What the hell were you thinking?" James said. "You're not that damn good, you fool!"

"But my hands…" Sebastian trailed off staring at his blue tinted hands, covered in charcoal.

"Come on man, we'll get out!" James said. "We'll find Argento."

"I don't care—I want to get to her!" Sebastian yelled, then slumped to the ground. "I have to save her!"

James paused. His friend, former boss, laid in a lump on the stone floor, heaving and shaking, his blue tinted hands covered in a layer of charcoal.

He slid to a seat beside him. "There's no reason to get excited." James laid his head back against the wall, a touch of charcoal smudging under his bright hair. "Sebastian, she survived his capture before, and she seems like a smart girl." Sebastian shuttered again. "Honestly, man, I'd no idea she meant this much. I knew you two were…but I thought you'd—we'd—left home because of your father."

Sebastian chuckled. "He'd have sold my paintings, each one

buying another plot of earth to till, more Parisian wine for his wife. Then they force away the girl I—” Sebastian stopped. “He forced me, James. Left me no choice. I am so sorry,” Sebastian sighed. “If I'd kept a cooler head, we'd be sitting at Mac's right now with an ale and a laugh. This damn insane place!”

“My God, Sebastian, this place is beautiful! It amazes me...” James' voice trailed off as he thought he sounded like a cheap philosopher and not the lowly thief he was. He shook his head and reached for the silver in his inner pocket. “I helped Kellogg steal this. I told him it was 'cause it'd help his little girl, and that's partly true. That little thing was turning into her papa—and me. But I wondered if a chunk of silver chains could help give us the upper hand, what with you being the artist's apprentice and all. But I also stole it for me. I knew I could. This was more than some silverware or trinkets from your father's house.” Sebastian snorted, but didn't look upset.

“This was a challenge,” James continued. He held up the strands and spun them in the lantern light. The light reflected against the jail cell walls. “You may not see it, but this is beautiful, not because of its silver color, but because I earned it...well, I beat the challenge.”

Sebastian laughed. “You certainly did run fast!” He punched James' arm.

“You and me both...”

"True." Sebastian flicked one of the strands and watched the light dance across the walls. "I see the beauty in this place. You should have seen the sky the night we got here—I've never seen anything more beautiful." He saw Anna's face in his mind for a brief second. "I bet it was more fantastic than that aurora thing the sailors from the north would talk about." The strand slowed its rocking and now spun slightly.

"But all I can think about is her," he faltered, as if the mention of Anna made it possible that she was in real trouble, "and that son of a bitch with the tattooed face. I have to help her, with Argento..."

James scooped up the silver and returned it to his pocket, and let out a long breath. "You and I been through worse. I'd think we can get outta here!"

"What you yelling about in there?" a guard dressed in all black, with the bizarre white mask hanging from his neck, questioned. He was tall and wide, not the sort James would want to meet in the cave, though he most likely already had.

Just like the past two days, the guard unlocked the gate and dropped a plate of toast on the ground, calling Sebastian a thief.

"So you still trying to say you're an artist?" The guard pointed at the smudged drawing on the wall.

"He is," James whispered.

"Ah, so you got something to say today? Good thing—the

Lady wishes to speak to you." The guard grabbed James by the collar, yanking him out into the hall.

"Wait a damn minute!" Sebastian scrambled to his feet.

"Just sit and enjoy yer breakfast, thief!" He shoved Sebastian back to the ground, letting out a cracked laugh.

James could hear Sebastian's voice echoing down the corridor as he was marched along by the Belvedere guardsman. The guard's laughing faded, and he was led to the end of the upward sloping corridor until they came to an iron door. The guard unlocked it, and they stepped onto an ornate suspension bridge. The metalwork was fine and strong, but slippery as James had wondered days before. The wind gusted across the expanse between the building and the rest of Castle Belvedere. James tried not looking down, and the guard laughed from his belly as James clutched onto the handrailing. "Move," he sneered. The smell of effervescent minerals filled James' nose as he tried taking a calming breath. He'd never been so high above anything. Below he could see the lower city, the streets wove in and out, black sandstone and golden flecks. Alleyways, and people moving to and fro, with the misleading aqueducts crossing the squares. He focused on the end of the bridge, letting the beat of the waterfall's crashing time his footsteps.

At the end, the guardsman pushed open yet another iron door, this one with a brass doorknob and workings, and was led to the main floor of Castle Belvedere. James memorized the layout of the castle much better than the darkened caves—easier in daylight for certain.

Up a staircase and through a large hall. They marched past rooms and other corridors, forced to turn by a shove. James realized that most of the rooms had their doors wide open, but the only people they came across were other guards. One room was full of a multitude of mirrors, another portraits. They passed a corridor that was lit with green hanging lamps, and one small study with a metal desk. Through an ornately carved mahogany door he spied soft velvet chairs and a table with a tea set. As they marched the guard swung open a door with a pink glass window and James was shoved through into a greenhouse. The muggy air was such a shock that he shuttered and then soaked in the clean dampness. Lush greenery lined the walls and strange vines draped down from the ceiling. Red, orange, pink, and purple flowers swayed in a planter to his left.

"Keep moving," the guard grunted and shoved James away from the flowers and to another door, this one with an orange glass window. He swung it and they stepped outside.

"You are called James," she stated. Lady Gioconda was standing at the far end of the enclosed garden, tending a trailing vine that crept up the golden wall. The mid-morning sun shone bright on the crushed granite pathways and silky rosemary bushes—their oils glistening back the sunlight.

"Yes, milady," James whispered, his voice had suddenly dried up. Perhaps it was the cold morning air after the humidity of the greenhouse. He cleared his throat as she waved him over.

"Thank you, Maurice. You are dismissed." The guard bowed and left them. "Tell me, James, are you familiar with this vine? I was told you worked at an estate in the land you are from."

He squinted at the vine but shook his head. "No, I don't know this one. Though I was assigned to the house, not the yards at the Albright's—" James cut himself off, realizing how easy it would be to keep rambling on, and unsure why. The Lady seemed so easy to speak to, to carry on a normal conversation. He reminded himself she was his jailer.

"What items did you take from the estate you worked at, James," Lady Gioconda asked, going about pruning the vine.

"Oh, uh, I never..." James stammered. Lady Gioconda turned to him and tilted her head, her eyes telling him she knew quite well, and that lying would not work.

"Silver, mostly," James admitted.

"Ah, silver. I prefer gold, yet that is neither here nor there. What if I made a deal with you, a trade? For one strand of the silver you carry in your inner vest pocket"—James' eyes went wide at this—"I will give you something you've already been accused of having illegally: a lump of peregrinite."

James' face twisted.

"Do not worry," she chuckled, "it is not being planted on you to prove anything. That is not how things are done here—we have a more…honest way. Honesty above all things.”

James reached into the inner pocket of his vest and nimbly untangled a strand of silver from the mass of braids. He picked one for her—not too thin, yet not the thickest either, but one expertly braided he could tell by simple touch. He pulled it out and offered it to her, the morning light glinting off the polished metal.

“So we have a bargain, James.” She offered a small black pouch from her pocket and dropped it into his hand. He felt something small, the size of a sugar cube, inside.

“It is very lovely.” She lifted the strand up in the light. “Made by artists, no doubt. Where was its destination when you acquired it?”

James coughed, “Oh, um, the shopkeeper said—”

“Don’t lie, James.”

He blushed. “I don’t know where it was going to, but it was from a place called Spain.”

“Spain. Interesting. Well now it will be a memory for me, of you.” She placed the strand into a pocket of her black dress. “Since you are not from Belvedere, nor even the surrounding lands as Duke Weldon has told me, you are unfamiliar with our city and our history. In the lower city, there is a section called Thieves Town,” she began to explain, skipping over the mention of Argento, and grasping the leaves of the vine again and slipping the dead parts off with delicate strokes of her knife. “A misnomer, perhaps, as there are many who frequent there who are not at all cunning in legerdemain. And some of the most entertaining theatrical shows are performed in Thieves Town. I regret not being able to visit them anymore, but my face is much too well known." She smiled again, and snipped off another dead branch.

"But it is truth that thieves settled that area of our city. Indeed, we have an interesting history with that type here. It is humorous that my guards labeled your friend as such, not knowing that you were the true one!" She laughed, small and short, almost tired. "James, you have a natural skill that some spend many a year perfecting," she began again.

"Excuse me, milady." The guardsman, Maurice, appeared behind them at the doorway.

"Ah, yes. Bring him in."

Maurice nodded and turned back out the door.

Lady Gioconda took James' arm. "My dear, would you please be so kind as to wait here?" She led him behind a large topiary of rosemary. The scent of the herb was potent in the air around a small, hidden bench.

"Of course, milady." James had fallen into the language of the others in the city. It was simple to do since she commanded respect, he thought. She nodded and walked off to her seat in the larger rosemary patch, where she had sat when they first met her. Only a few feet off from his own spot, he watched as she took her seat, lifted her garden knife and began to cut the rosemary from the closest bush.

"Milady." Maurice returned. "Here is Simon, as requested." A second guard appeared behind him.

"Thank you, Maurice. You may leave us."

She looked at her guard. "You look weary, Simon. Please have a seat." She patted the empty place beside her once and moved the basket of sliced rosemary stems to her right.

Simon hesitated. The white mask dangling from his neck was bright against his black tunic, the eyes low, empty black slits.

"Many thanks, madam." Simon nodded and took a seat on the bench. "I am honored."

Lady Gioconda resumed plucking the rosemary. "In my youth, many said I seemed to have a sixth sense—that I seemed to know things, or at least looked as if I knew something." She smiled ever so slightly.

Simon fidgeted, crossing his legs then changing his mind.

"Simon. Would you like me to lie to you? Should I pretend I do not know where it is you have been going? That I am unaware of the Dali and the events that have taken place there? Would it make it easier?"

Simon's chest heaved as he took a shallow breath.

"There is a part of me that wishes we both could attribute it to the Harlequin Man's charm." Simon was shaking. "But we know it was the gold."

Simon was frozen to his seat.

"That man killed many in his service, to that I say nothing. Yet, betrayal requires penalty."

And with that she raised her silver knife and with one swift cut sliced Simon across the throat. He grabbed his neck and tumbled to the ground. Blood pooled around his head on the golden gravel as he flailed, gasping and twitching.

"But that man killed innocents—friends, good men, and keeps a young woman as his own trophy. Gold indeed."

Simon could not respond. His eyes had grown wide in his last throws. The Lady Gioconda stood from her bench, the small knife, his death warrant, in her hands, and his blood dripping down the rosemary stalks.

James was breathing hard from behind the topiary.

Chapter 21

The sound of feet marching in the hallway pulled Sebastian away from the image on the wall. It still wasn't right, not how he saw it in his mind's eye. Sebastian tossed the charred table leg aside, causing a sharp clang against the stones under the half-moon window. Rain had begun to fall moments before and the first drips were coming down from the ledge.

"You've not convinced us you're an artist, thief," the growl from behind snarked. At the bars of the cell stood the guard, mask still hanging down, and James beside him. His friend's eyes looked dark and empty—it was one Sebastian had only witnessed in his friend as he stood at the edge of the mirror pond looking up at the unfamiliar skies.

"What did you do to him?" Sebastian growled back at the guard. The man sneered, and shoved James into the cell. James stumbled and landed on the lower bunk of the bed.

"Are you all right? What happened? Where'd they take you?" Sebastian shot question after question at James. He pulled a ragged blanket off the other bunk and draped it on James' shoulders, then handed him a tin cup filled with rainwater he'd gathered from the half-moon window.

"Argento is dead." The water sloshed once, dripping on the floor, then was still.

Sebastian sneered. "What?"

James looked up into his friend's face. The darkness in James' eyes was the feeling of truth, and death.

"That woman...she slit a guard across the throat!" The water cup in his hand trembled, small rings bounced on the surface. Sebastian took the cup from him, but it shook more in his own hands.

"We have to get out of here!" He spun over to the plastered wall, the graffiti of his woodland scene still fresh. Sebastian inched along the wall with the burnt table leg, adding bits of charcoal to parts, rubbing and smoothing other parts with his glowing blue hands, perfecting the image was the only way.

"Wait." James was standing, the blanket off his shoulders. His right hand was palm up, in it was a small opaque blue lump, no bigger than a peach pit.

Sebastian only looked for a moment and snatched the lump from James' hand. He stepped back to the bars and tilted his head to the left, eyes shifting slowly across the image. He nodded, then began on the left of the wall, inching along again, moving the lump in smooth soft circles, shading the image in raw peregrinite. No color dust was left by the lump, but the artist could sense it changing— even James' thieving hands could feel a cool breeze, he began to smell oak.

"Let's go."

Sebastian started to hand the lump of peregrinite—hardly

diminished by his use—back to James but he shook his head. Sebastian nodded and placed it into his own pocket. Backing up against the bars, Sebastian breathed deep, lowered his shoulders and sprinted for the image.

The woods were alive with winter birdsong. Above James' head, perched on a branch, was a small red bird. He'd have called it a cardinal, but something told him Argento would have corrected him.

Argento.

James sat up and scrambled to his feet, spinning around in the piles of fallen oak leaves. He felt—fine. He barely remembered awaking on this side before, only vague images and small ideas, the night sky, wind. Yet this time he felt alert and normal. As James searched the area for Sebastian he thought how this drawing, while good as Sebastian's always are, was nowhere near as good as the castle one he'd painted—or even his sea painting.

He walked around the large oak tree and found that he was not in a forest, but an orchard filled with fruit trees. Though most were bare, one row held small blue fruit he didn't recognize. At the end of the row of fruit trees, he came to a tiny farmhouse. The whitewashed walls in the afternoon light looked warm and inviting. For a moment, he wished to be standing on the Albright's estate, tending the grounds, trimming the hedges, and caring for the animals. Though in truth, he spent more time in the house with his master at lessons, or traipsing about the town.

His wave of nostalgia broke as he came upon Sebastian knocked out against the south wall of the farmhouse's barn.

"Wake up!" he shouted at Sebastian, who only mumbled something. "Come on, get up!" James grabbed him under the shoulders and lifted him to his feet. Together, they stumbled into the open doors of the barn.

A shaft of warm winter sunlight flooded the doorway of the barn. The smell of hay and animals hit his nose.

"I don't hear rain," Sebastian mumbled from the spot James had laid him, in the sunny patch. James scrambled about the stables gathering tack.

"No, it's sunny here. Very cheerful, I'd say, sir." James slipped in his haste, but Sebastian didn't seem to hear. James grabbed a second saddle and opened the gates of two stalls. He led out two horses.

"Sebastian." He tapped his face, then smacked him.

"Sonofabitch!" Sebastian shouted and slurred.

"Good, you're awake. Come on, we have to go before the farmer notices his horses are gone."

When the farmer returned later to his barn, he found two sparkling silver chains in his empty horse stalls.

The night came fast as the horses' hooves, and it was midnight when they pulled the reins and stopped their horses, the blue glow of Sebastian's hands blinding them.

Argento was dead.

They'd been riding for two days. The first day was nothing but a blur. They'd gone east towards Weldon. A stand of sweeping junipers lined the northern horizon. The spindles rose high into the pale sky, vultures perched atop some as they rode on.

They were in an open field, dotted with haystacks—the rounded piles dark shadows as the night approached, seeming secretive and transient. But leaning against one for a few hours was better than lying out in the open for Belvedere guards, or worse, to find them, Sebastian figured.

Argento was dead.

While Sebastian sat in the dark shadow of the haystack and leaned against the straw, he stared out at the line of junipers. They massed into one jagged black shape on the horizon, wild teeth ripping at the star-filled purple sky. He hadn't seen the night sky in a week after riding in a storm the day before, and it still shocked him how strange they looked. These constellations were not the Big Dipper or Cassiopeia. Argento had called one the blue guitar.

"Anna," Sebastian mumbled. He found the coin was in his hands, the wooden carvings looking blue in the blue glow.

"What?" James asked. He'd started a small fire a safe distance from the pile of straw, even though it smelled damp from yesterday's rains.

Sebastian shook his head. "Nothing."

Argento was dead.

The fields of royal thyme gradually grew more and more pronounced as they rode on the next morning. It was the first glimmer of hope Sebastian had felt for ages. As they galloped across the empty fields of wildflowers and tall grasses, the skies grew darker behind them, until the entire sun-filled sky was blotted out with churning clouds. The first drop hit him in the face, and he scowled, pressing his head downward into the winds. James on the other hand turned his face upwards, inhaling the clean air.

By darkening twilight they saw the first turret of Weldon. He'd remembered how the orange glow had stood out from the blue shadows when he'd seen it the week before, and the pale harlequin flag fluttering above it. Yet now there was only a dot of yellow, perhaps a candle on the windowsill, and the flag was straight out in the wind.

He wanted to believe she was there, looking out the window, watching the two riders approaching her castle-prison.

But Argento was dead—only they could help her now.

~~~~~

Anna saw them, only for a moment—two riders approaching Weldon from the west. The sun had set and darkness stretched away on the fields and the river crossing. Low, dark growling thunder
~~~~~

echoed across the open plains, almost impossible to hear, and she thought it was in her jostled mind, but it sounded like wildcats. She leaned forward against the glass, unfolding the window, and the growling howl grew fast. The door behind her opened, mixing the low growl with the dry screech of the hinges. His man was there, a new one she did not recognize, but knew it was his henchmen by the overt colored diamond patches on his shoulder. The man jolted two steps into her room and gripped her upper arm. Her reaction was perfect—she leaned away sheltering her bruised face from his heavy one, so much like the drunkard at Senora's Cantina; he even smelled of liquor. He snickered once, though that was all she needed. Knowing that out there, on the Weldon plains were two riders not carrying the Harlequin Man's standard lit something in her gut.

On the windowsill was the glass statue of the woman holding a book. It was made of the same green glass as the glasses in Senora's Cantina, and with a stance that exuded independence. Anna's hands were hot and she'd started to sweat. The thought that the glass would slip through her grip flashed in her mind, but too fast to change it. With this smelly man's grip on her right upper arm, she gripped the figure, and shifted her weight against her injured left foot, pivoted only a bit, and swung the heavy glass statue across her, connecting with the smelly man's skull. She felt the glass connect, and the backwards push of her weight bouncing to her back foot. She remembered the way her walking staff had been caught in the back streets of Spain by the cloaked stranger—Grandad—who'd begged to pay her passage to England. He claimed to be doing penance for his past failures. Anna now felt she knew why.

But now, this smelly loyal servant of Knell was crumpled in a pile on her floor, her pretty woven rug rumpled up under his large form. Anna felt this one chance at her escape fading with every breath, slinking away into shadowy corners. Her heart wasn't beating as fast as she thought it would be, but she shuffled that thought away as she fumbled for the door key on the loyal henchman's belt.

The tower room was an oasis of joy in her youth, perhaps someday again, her mind raced as she ran down flight after flight of stairs. Hope was blooming, she felt it deep in her gut in shades of bright yellow and purple like the royal thyme, and deep blue like Sebastian's ocean painting of sand and salt. Anna's cracked lips slipped into a sliver of a smile. She could barely feel her feet as they ran down the stone floors of the corridors, past the closed dining hall doors where once great light poured down through the stained-glass ceiling of yellow and blue, out of the hall and into the kitchens where the door, her freedom and escape, was there for the taking.

Where Victor Knell sat in the catacombs eating roasted goose.

Chapter 22

Claude rose from his bed. A meal of salmon, cheese, and bread sat on his side table, a pot of black tea steaming next to it.

He stretched, then sipped.

In the corner, on a blue velvet poof sat Sabine, her whiskers twitching in anticipation of her morning cream saucer. Claude set it next to the furry companion and she purred with thanks and luxury.

On another table were stacks of wide manuals, each with specific colors and techniques.

Claude stepped to the small yellow tinted window. Outside the tall grasses swayed and birds flitted by in shades of ocher.

On the wall next to the window was a long parchment. Dashes lined over and over in long rows. Claude reached down to the table and picked up a long wooden dowel that tapered to a point at one end. He dipped the point into a pot of ebony ink next to the open manual depicting a forearm and the layers of muscles and innards.

Wiping the drips carefully on the edge of the pot, Claude stood tall and with a graceful motion, swiped the dowel against the hanging parchment, leaving another dash.

Sabine wove between Claude's feet, her purr louder than before. Claude turned to stroke her soft grey fur when his eye caught something out of place on his table. Leaning against a leather manual labeled *Practices of the Ancient Marks* was a scrap of paper:

Noon.

Many thanks, Master.
VK

Claude reread the note. He then paced slowly to the corner of his room, the one always in shadow, and pulled out an odd chair, the back of which was on a hinge. Lying it back, and sitting on a stool, he dragged his manual table next to it, and set out three pots of colored ink—white, black, and red.

Sighing deeply, Claude stood and shuffled to the yellow window and yanked the parchment from the wall.

~~~~~~

The rain let loose, pouring large drops on Sebastian and James as they reined in their panting horses. Mud caked their boots and pants, splattered up from the pounding hooves across the open plain.

Winds swelled up, chilling the sweat on Sebastian's neck. He shivered and swung fast off his horse and up to the solid oak door. Sebastian raised his arm, about to pound on the door, when James whistled.

"Look." He pointed down a road leading away from Weldon. Only two hundred yards down the path a carriage pulled away—a
~~~~~~

swath of yellow blinked across the windowpane, visible against the dullness of twilight, and the darkness of the clouds.

"We're too late, he's taken her someplace!" Sebastian cursed, his growl lifting on the winds.

A figure leapt out of the open doorway and laid a punch in Sebastian's gut. A whisper of air gusted out. James leaned back against his horse and pushed forward at the figure's back, laying one jab in the man's kidney. The attacker arched forward, then swung wide against James, but he ducked.

"Where'd he take her?" Sebastian exhaled as much as he could with hardly any breath. Knell's henchman snickered and spun back around. His tunic was painted in red, white, and black diamonds, and his black breeches faded into the lowering light.

"That bitch is done for. She's getting what she deserves! No one betrays Lord Knell."

Sebastian charged towards the henchman letting out a primal scream. The harlequin colors spun, and the henchman rammed his fist into Sebastian's head. The young artist dropped like a lump to the mud.

A blue haze was all around, a cloudy haze, muffled sounds like a foggy morning in a wood. His mind was scoured of all thoughts and images. Save one.

It was Anna. She was sitting in a grey field of dead grasses. All around her were the carcasses of sheep, each one shorn of its wool and left to starve. He started to walk towards her, his feet catching on the dried thatch and stumbling on the dead sheep.

The closer he came to his Anna, the blue haze began to lift. His eyes tried to focus on her face but they were drawn to her odd clothes.

She reached up her arms to him when he saw the marks. Anna was covered head to toe in black, red, and white diamonds. Her skin was livid and burning along the tattoo lines.

And she was screaming—her blistering cry swept across the empty field.

Sebastian clapped his hands on his ears but her wail penetrated into his skull.

"God! No!"

Anna still reached out to him, her scream begging for help, or mercy.

"Anna!" Sebastian screamed.

"Sebastian!" James was shaking him.

"Stop!"

"No, you stop! You have to stop yelling or more of those henchmen will find us."

He could taste the scent of minerals that hung in the air. Sitting up, he grabbed James' collar.

"She's burning, he's mutilated her!"

James pried Sebastian's hand off his shirt. "No, that was a

dream. You got knocked out."

"No, dammit. It was real. That bastard did something to her."

James helped him sit up. "Just breathe, all right?"

Sebastian looked around. They were in some kind of catacomb or crypt. It appeared to be flooded with spring rains. There was only one dry spot left—right behind the door. Any further in and they would be sitting in the waters. An oil lamp was burning on the stone floor, the light extending the cavernous feel. Yet, the worst part of the crypt wasn't the water or the darkness. It was the lone statue in the center of the waters. The figure held a bowl, its head turned down as if gazing in. Sebastian figured it might have been some god or even an elemental of sorts. To James, the statue seemed to be looking into the bowl as if for an answer.

Even from down in these catacombs they could hear the storm raging, thunder shook Weldon down past its foundations, and the pool around them rippled like wine in a glass when a person stomps by.

"When the storm moves on, we will leave," James explained. "A serving girl took us here. She said Knell took Anna in his carriage before we arrived. The girl told me where they were going."

"That tattooed son of a bitch." Sebastian sighed and leaned back against the wall. "With Argento dead..."

"He'll pay." It was cliché, yet Sebastian was glad to hear his friend say it.

By the fourth hour, much of the heavy rains had passed.

A ledge wrapped along one side of the room, almost the same height as the waters. The thin stone jutted out enough for them to shuffle foot over foot along the wall. Bricked-in archways belied former windows, and the long term settling of Weldon House.

The serving girl told James of a small hatch on the far wall, one her lady had used the first time she had left Weldon. Sebastian grinned as he and James wadded out into the water and spun the bowl in the hands of the statue, forcing open a small doorway on the northern wall. Beyond, in the misty morning light, were their horses—tied to a stump surrounded by violets.

Chapter 23

In a matter of hours, sand drifts began to overtake the grassy plains. Grit and dust flew into Sebastian and James' faces, and they covered their noses with their shirts. At noon the sun came out and plastered them with a blast of late winter heat, the kind that causes you to stretch and breath deep and comfortably after the cold air of deep winter.

As the last tuft of grass went by, they came upon a boulder, massive in size and quite out of place for the arid empty landscape. Sebastian reigned in his horse.

"Let's go on foot from here," he said as he dismounted his horse.

"Why? We haven't any idea how far he is."

"I have an idea it's not too much farther off—Argento told me about the Dali, and this is the entry." He led his horse around the side of the boulder and tied him to a smaller boulder sitting at the base.

The landscape was empty and grey, and constantly shifting sand dunes on the west and east left a salt-flat of empty hard pan between. Argento had said there were storms in this place, bizarre out of nowhere gusting winds, kicking up dirt and salt. That dry lightning could appear in the Saltstorm Vortex, and the old man himself had fallen victim to the power of that lightning, when

Knell's traveling device had harnessed the storm.

Sebastian understood why people of this land associated Terry's Flat with death and fear—he felt the bleached empty scent of it in his throat.

However, he understood its beauty as well. The strange calm yet movement was interesting. He wished he was here for other reasons so he could attempt to capture it on canvas.

They walked along a dry barren road that was barely visible, trudging and kicking up the sand as they went. They couldn't tell how far they had gone as the emptiness made distance hard to track, though from time to time they would pass hunks of driftwood or old trees. It seemed as if time itself melted into the sands.

"Oh sweet Lord! Anna!" Sebastian stopped and stared.

No more than fifty feet away was a mass of discarded logs and sticks. The pile was tall, more than ten feet at the zenith, and was built on the top of a platform of rocks that seemed to be morphing in shape.

Atop the pile of wood, in the middle like an ornament, sat Anna. Her legs dangled off the edge. Her face was battered and blood caked under her nose. Her dress of yellow was splattered in red—it was vibrant and easy to see against the grey of the twisted land. Anna straightened taller to see them. She was shouting something, but they couldn't hear.

Below the pyre—for that is what Sebastian realized it to be—

sat Victor Knell. The Harlequin Man was every bit as evil and disturbing as he'd been described: a twisted, elegant man, the red diamonds on his face vibrant as the blood on Anna's dress. Next to him, leaning against the rocks was a long silver staff, the white glare of the Dali gleaming off its polished shine.

"Well, isn't this lovely?" Knell pondered aloud. Sebastian and James were grabbed by two henchmen, each wearing their master's harlequin pattern along their sleeves. Sebastian bucked against his captor. His head exploded in hot fire when the man slammed his shoulder into Sebastian's ear, igniting the pain from the night before. Through his half-closed eyes he watched James ram an elbow into his holder's ribs, but the henchman held him fast.

Scurrying out from behind the rocky mound came another trio of Knell's men, each with a mace in his hand. Knell acknowledged each with a flick of his head, and each returned their deference with a fist across their chest and a nod.

"Now that you have settled down, I will continue. You are the apprentice of the *former* Duke of Weldon, I believe. And you," he gestured at James, "are his bondsmen?" James struggled against the henchman.

"You each no doubt will tell me how you want the girl. I can understand why, she is quite...striking." Knell leaned back against the rock face and tilted his head towards Anna. His grin widened, pulling the marks on his cheeks up and out, stretching the diamonds against their grain. "Yet, are you sure you still want her?" Knell returned his gaze to the men. "After all, she is no longer, shall we say, 'unmarked'?"

Knell reached up his hand and slapped Anna's ankle. She gasped and let out a low moan. She shivered and her legs trembled. Anna pulled herself higher up the pile, her arms quaking as she pulled her body higher up, not letting her ankle make contact with the rough wood. She fought the urge to scream out, fighting herself and the pain with every inch she climbed.

"You bastard," Sebastian sneered. The henchman holding him swung wide and socked him across the jaw. The fire in his temples flared again. Blood dribbled down his lips—he spat it at Knell's feet.

Knell laughed, his voice muffled in the salty winds. "Ah! The young apprentice loves the maiden, how perfect!" Knell sprung up, taking only three steps and stopping inches from Sebastian. "You have no idea how much I will enjoy watching you be pummeled to death. You and your slave boy here. The last of the former duke's men." Knell backhanded him, a blur of colors erupting in Sebastian's eyes.

"Sebastian!" James yelled, but was punched in the gut by his holder.

A whirl of brown streaked from the corner of his eye, and the henchman with the mean punch was slammed to the ground.

"What the hell?" James eked out, the wind knocked out of him. Knell's guards spread about searching for the source of the lone arrow. Each one scoured the blinding sands for the archer, but nothing could be seen. Sebastian struggled against his captor, but the henchman only tightened his grip on his wrists.

"We fight for your honor, Duke of Weldon!" a voice called out from the west. In the distance Sebastian saw a black figure standing atop Terry's Stone. The pale white face almost aglow against the blackness of his cloak. The archer raised his bow again, taking aim in their direction.

"Get him!" Knell screamed. His eyes were wide, not in shock but in rage. His nose flared and his stance was hunched and ready as if to pounce himself.

Across the sands came a swath of white mixed with black, flowing capes aloft in the winds. Leading the charge of approaching swordsmen was the black and gold standard of Belvedere, next to the flag of Weldon.

"No!" Knell growled and slunk back against the rock pile. He began to climb up the rocks, springing each level like an acrobat. Sebastian looked for Anna but could no longer see her. In his mind she was hiding in a crevice of one of the rocks. If there had been time and space he would have painted her an escape route.

He felt the hold on his wrists loosen, and turned behind him to see his holder collapse to the ground. Sebastian stared at the crumpled henchman, contorted strangely in the sands, a white dust puffed up from where he hit the sands.

"How can we reach her?" Argento inquired.

"What the hell?" Sebastian blurted. "How..." In the brightness of the sands his silver hair glowed even whiter than the blue hands, blowing in the winds, frizzed and large.

"Argento!" James yelled.

"Yes, James, even I."

"How..." Sebastian began.

"Quickly! Before Knell can set it ablaze!" Argento pointed to the pyre of branches set atop the rock formation. "No time to explain, Master Albright!"

Argento pushed him towards the pyre. They ran, dodging in and out and around the harlequin patterns and white masks. Mace clashed with sword, blood mixed with white sands. He briefly thought he saw Anna's face peek out from the top of the pyre, but lost sight of her as one of Knell's men swung his mace at him. He and James clobbered him, sending the henchman into the hands of two Belvedere swordsmen who finished him off properly.

They reached the bottom of the morphing rocks. Arrows whirred past the agile body of Victor Knell as he scoured the face of the rocks, even as they changed shape around him. Argento began to climb followed by Sebastian. Another harlequin henchman attacked James, who wrestled him to the ground.

"Ah! Dear Duke! I should have let the Flat make dust and bones out of you!" Knell yelled down at them. "This one betrayed me," he pointed up to where Sebastian had seen Anna. "And even if I were to let her live—which I have decided not to—each step she would have taken would remind her that I follow. I think that's poetic, do you not?" Knell's face was distorted, nostrils flared and lip curled. "And you—the new one with the mark of the artist—no worries. I heard tell that losing love and gaining tragedy is inspiration for art. You're welcome."

"You will burn for this, Knell!" Argento called.

"I am tired of dealing with you." Knell ripped a stone and raised it above his head. "There will be no doubt who is the Duke, now."

The stone dropped from Knell's hands, landing with a crack on Argento's forehead. His grip lost, he fell back to the sands with a thud, his silver hair splayed around, the blood covering his face.

All sounds vanished. There was only the sound of blood thumping in Sebastian's ears. He turned his head up to Knell who hung off the rock face with one arm, the other still dangling where he'd dropped the rock. The diamond pattern morphed like the rocks—slow and stylized—into a grin and chuckle.

But with Argento lying crumpled at the foot of the pyre, blood covering his face, and James laying punch after punch on a henchman, kicking up the sands of this desert, Sebastian's rage engulfed him.

Sebastian jumped up, his arms raised, clutching onto Knell's ankle. The look of utter shock on Knell's face enticed Sebastian to pull, and he tumbled to the ground, landing on his knees and howling in pain.

Sebastian dropped from the rocks. He lunged, sucker punching Knell in the throat. Sebastian felt the Adam's apple between his knuckles. The pain was extreme in his fist, but the hit was true. He was joking no more. No snarky remarks from Master Albright. Not this time.

Knell coughed as he dropped full force on his back. The hasty and elegant movements of before gone as he flailed in the dust.

Sebastian scrambled to hold Knell down. He grabbed hold of the traveling device, which he realized was a kind of lightning rod, as it leaned at the base of the morphing rocks and slammed it against Knell's chest.

Knell was stunned still. How could he have miscalculated?

"What, you bastard? Nothing else to say now? How dare you?" Sebastian yelled in the other man's face. "Oh, I'm sorry, are you uncomfortable here, with this lightning rod, hmm?" Sebastian pressed the device harder. "Well, good thing we've got this peregrinite then. Maybe it's time you took a little trip like the others."

Sebastian was yelling now. He reached into his pocket and

pulled the minerals out. He dropped them slowly through his fingers like hourglass sands. They were so pure they glowed blue even in the harsh bright light of the Dali.

"How about taking a trip, you bastard?"

Knell's eyes grew large, stretching the tattoos wide and distorted.

"Wait!" someone shouted.

Sebastian stopped.

"Young man, you cannot do that, as much as it would give me pleasure to see him sent wandering." Lady Gioconda had stepped out of an elegant black and gold coach, her guard Maurice sword drawn and eyes watchful. She glided over to Knell and Sebastian.

"She's right!" It was Anna. She was breathing hard, sitting in the dust by Argento's twisted frame. Sebastian's mouth dropped down, his gut tightened. Her black eye dark and purple, the broken nose swollen. Her dress was ripped where she'd dragged herself across the hardpan, her bare legs covered in a fine layer of silt.

Her foot contorted to one side where the ankle was swelling. And on that broken ankle wrapped a ring of red, black, and white diamond tattoos.

"Are you admiring my work, Artist?" Knell croaked from under the weight of the traveling device.

"Bastard!" Sebastian screamed.

"Sebastian! Please!" Anna was pushing herself up to her feet with the aid of a large stick from the pyre. James had rushed to her side, but took a long glance at Argento's still form. "He'll end up in your world somewhere, doing God knows what. We cannot risk that." Anna was gasping between her words. Images of the Sisters of Colina del Rojo and of Kellogg and little Maisie, even Sebastian's parents, swam through their minds.

"Time for all things, milady," Knell's voice nimble in its meaning, unabashedly leering at Anna.

"Silence, demon," Lady Gioconda whispered at him, and Sebastian pushed his knee down harder on his chest.

"You are the pinnacle of duplicity, Lady Gioconda!" Knell spat.

Anna limped over, stumbling on a stone and Sebastian jumped up. The quick glance from her eyes telling him all he needed to know.

Knell took this chance, darting his arm out and grabbing a pale yellow stone.

"No! I have had enough of your tricks." Anna raised the stick above her head and swung down.

A sound like wind in a tunnel, hollow and fast, escaped Knell's body when the stick landed on his stomach. His face contorted, spreading the tattoos wide. A splintery crack of ribs accompanied the sound, and he was knocked unconscious.

Relief and exhaustion spread over Anna and she crumpled

against Sebastian. He helped her to the ground, and she shook with emotion. His hand stroked her hair.

All around them the Belvedere guardsmen were busy tying up an unconscious Harlequin Man and loading him into a black coach after a subtle hand gesture from Lady Gioconda.

"You learn that in Spain?" Sebastian whispered, a smile on his face.

She dropped her head down against him and let a laugh trickle out. "Where else, my love," she said through a tear and laugh filled explosion. He lifted her face and kissed her.

The aftermath of the bizarre fight felt slow and unreal. Behind them, the morphing stones continued to shift and change shape. James watched as the wind of the Dali shifted sand into the puddles of blood. Knell's men were scattered about the area, left to be carrion or returned to the dust from which they came. A few Belvedere guardsmen had also perished, but their comrades were taking them back to be laid to rest in their homeland. James swallowed and could taste the blood from a few good punches laid on him. Maurice, Lady Gioconda's bodyguard, gave James a respectful nod, which he returned.

"I already have enough of a headache, Master Albright," Argento let out a moan of sorts as he sat up, a hand to his head.

"Duke Weldon? Are you ok?" James asked him, helping him to his feet.

"You can still call me Argento, my boy." He smiled at the thief. "Anna!"

Sebastian picked her up and carried her to him.

"Grandad." She wrapped her arms around her grandfather. She could smell the familiar scent of his paints still on his vest. "I tried so hard to find you. And then you'd found me. Grandad, it is all right." She wiped a tear from Argento's wrinkled face. For the first time he looked like life had made its mark. "We are home."

He nodded, unable to speak.

"Annalisa." Lady Gioconda was by their side. "I am overjoyed to have you back in these lands. I will want to know all about your times, but now I must return to Belvedere. I have an imp to deposit in a dungeon." She gave Anna one of her signature smiles.

"Thank you so much, godmother." Anna hugged her, too. Sebastian looked at James who just shrugged.

"Take care of my cousin, Annalisa." Lady Gioconda kissed Argento on each cheek, then signaled her men to depart.

"Cousin?" Sebastian asked Argento, raising an eyebrow. Dust kicked up from the guardsmen's horses and they all squinted against the sand.

"Playing your games as usual, Grandad?" Anna laughed, leaning on her stick as Sebastian helped them both towards the one coach left. James had jumped up to the rumble seat, readying the horses. With tender steps Anna and Argento got into the coach.

"Mystery is art," the Duke of Weldon expounded. Sebastian let out a loud sigh, and Argento laughed.

"What will she do with Knell?" James called down, remembering the way she had dealt with Knell's spy.

"One thing I have learned over the years is not to ask my cousin about her ways of dealing justice. It isn't worth the philosophical headache." Argento reached up to hold his head again.

"Let us go back home, Grandad. Weldon needs its Duke." She squeezed his hand.

The carriage rumbled across the salt flat.

~~~~~

"Tell me, Victor, did you know Annalisa's history? Did it ever come up while she stood as a prisoner in Weldon House? Did you ever hear her tell of her childhood? Of her time spent away in the land of many waterways, of black stones flecked with gold, the city on top of the peregrinite mines?" She raised an eyebrow in questioning.

Knell, who was perched on a rough wooden stool, slowly turned his eyes up to see Lady Gioconda standing in front of his cell, lit by the flickering light of the torches, and flanked on each side by her bodiless guards. She, dressed in her black garb touched in golden linings, looked much like the guards themselves with her delicate pale face radiating in the darkness of the cave. Like so many times
~~~~~

before, a slight smile played on the corner of her mouth.

"I take it from your silence that you never inquired more about the woman you coveted than what your lecherous imagination could conjure? How she was raised for a time as a child of Belvedere. She was a relation of the house of Gioconda." Knell's dark glance morphed like the changing stones of the Dali into a wide smile, stretched and jovial.

"Why no, milady, I'm afraid that Anna never spoke much. That is usually how I prefer the women I eventually take to my bed."

"Now, we both know that is not the truth. You simply were too lustful to hear her. But she heard you, saw you, knew your truth."

Knell snorted.

"If that were not the case, the Lady of Weldon would not have escaped you, correct?"

Knell's lip twitched and his nostrils flared, so obvious in his emotions. Lady Gioconda smiled again. Knell's body tightened. She watched as the muscles in his thighs and arms started to quake. The tattoos on his face, though dim in the murky light of his cell, twisted and shifted.

Knell jumped and his face was at the bars of his cell. Lady Gioconda did not move, not even a change in her expression as the tattooed man leaned against the bars, hands gripping them tight.

"You have quite the ways don't you, finding the places to poke at a man trapped in a cell, a prison. You have buried me alive.

Call me cruel, at least I had the decency of ending the lives of my enemies. Anna could have spent her life in my delights instead of that artist she's taken. She and you will spend the afterlife dancing in the fires like harlots!" Knell screamed.

Lady Gioconda's hand darted out from her pocket, the torch light gleamed off of her silver dagger as it ran smoothly through Knell's neck, slicing a series of the harlequin tattoos running down his right side. Shock filled his eyes, and rage, but there was no time for such thoughts. He grabbed his throat, and stumbled backwards, knocking over the stool, and scurrying backwards to the wall of the cell. His body twitched and spasmed, the focused movements of before gone.

Lady Gioconda turned her back to the cell and walked into the darkness.

Epilogue

The fog rolled into Port City off the sea, bringing the salt air and dropping it into the streets. Sylvia pulled her scarf closer to her nose and tightened her shawl. She bumped up off the seat as the cart rode over a loose stone in the cobbled road.

"Sorry, my love." Henry rubbed her shoulder. "Didn't see that rock." She patted his hand, but also her backside.

The cart slowed up in front of a small pub. Henry jumped down and around to help Sylvia from the cart. "I'll only be a little bit. I'll bring you a biscuit," she said.

She pecked him on the cheek and stepped into the pub.

It was dark inside, but after a moment her eyes adjusted. The place was bustling with patrons, most at tables as close to the large hearth as possible, escaping the cold outside. The bar was polished golden oak, which didn't match the grey weathered board walls.

A stocky man stood behind the bar, pulling on taps and serving strong scented coffee in mis-matched mugs.

Sylvia waddled towards the bar and the man trotted over to her and pulled out a stool.

"Missy, please have a seat."

Sylvia smiled. "I think I will." She took his hand and climbed slowly up, holding her stomach to keep her balanced. "Thank you, sir."

"Welcome to the Sliver Cup. What can I get ya?"

"Tea?"

"A'corse. Maisie!" he called to a young girl collecting mugs. "Bring this lass the spiced tea."

The girl nodded and spun over to a large teapot where she poured a large mug full of a dark liquid. The scent of anise and nutmeg filled the air.

"Thank you," Sylvia told the girl who smiled and dashed off. "She's yours?"

"Aye," Kellogg replied.

"So lovely." She sipped the strong tea.

"If it ain't too outta place me saying, but looks like it won't be long and you're own wee one'll be here?" The man smiled.

Sylva nodded and patted her stomach. "The midwife says another two months."

"Well, if it be a girl like my Maisie, better keep an extra eye out. True for the lads, but I only can speak to my own." He laughed and returned to the bar.

Sylvia sipped her tea and watched the people in the pub. She saw travelers in costumes from far off lands, and workers from the docks in heavy woolen coats. A man was reading a newspaper with his back to the roaring fire. One table laid out with mugs of spiced coffee and scones, a group of people laughed and clinked their mugs, and Sylvia imagined them later walking to the dock to disembark on a great journey on the seas, to adventure and romance. She then remembered Henry out in the cart and turned back to the man behind the bar.

"Pardon me, I'm looking for someone called Kellogg. He's supposed to have a package for me."

The man chuckled. "That'd be me, lass. So that'd make ye Mrs. Albright?"

Sylvia burst out laughing. She gripped onto the bar to keep from toppling off the stool.

"Lord, no," she managed through her laughter. From the moment she announced she was with child, Caroline Albright had banished her to the kitchens ("for your health, my dear"), then found errand after errand away from Albright Manor. This was just the latest one, but so far the furthest away. Henry had protested that she should not travel all the way to Port City in her delicate state, but Sylvia relished the idea of being away from Caroline's jealous stare.

Kellogg was staring at her when she finally gained her voice. "I am only Mrs. Albright's messenger."

"Ah. Seems out of the ordinary to send a lady in your state to travel," he paused but when she only smiled he continued, "but if you'll follow me, I'll show you it."

They walked through the pub to the back room. A group of men were sitting around at cards but Kellogg kicked them out.

"I had the winning hand, for certain!"

"Save yer bluffs for later, Murphy."

Once the card players left, Kellogg motioned to a stack of items against the back wall. Large crates with various stamps from around the world were stacked up in no particular order. A few of the boxes were colored on the sides with faded paint.

"Over here, lass." Kellogg pulled back a cream-colored canvas tarp to reveal a large oil painting.

There it was. Sand and seafoam, crashing blue waves and seagulls in the air. The grey sky and clouds swirling above the blue green sea. And the black image of a ship sailing off into the horizon.

Sylvia nodded. "That's the one by Master Sebastian Albright, for sure."

"Sketch was much more than he ever let on," Kellogg mumbled to himself with a smile and a shake of his head. Sylvia walked a few steps around the back room as he began to re-wrap the painting. She stopped when she saw a bit of bright yellow behind another painting.

It looked like a castle balcony, or a walkway she'd seen in a book once. On it were flower garlands and waving flags. It reminded her of a wedding, like her own but much more elaborate, like for a princess. The bride was wearing a pale yellow dress, which had caught her eye a moment ago, and had tiny yellow and purple flowers in her hair.

"Anna?" she whispered. She wasn't completely sure it was

her until she realized she also knew two other figures. Next to Anna, holding her hands was Master Albright, wearing blue gloves for some reason, and a glowing smile. Sebastian had the purple and yellow violets in his coat pocket. On the other side of Sebastion was James. Instead of his regular garb of a servant, he was head to toe in black, and what looked like a black cloak as well. The only person she didn't recognize was the older man standing near Anna. He looked somehow both regal and like a working man, and his hair was large and very white.

"Where did you get this?" she asked Kellogg, who was about to tie the ocean painting with rough twine.

Kellogg glanced over. "Came to me about six or so months ago on the *Horse Dawn*, last time it made port." He came and stood next to her and they both gazed down at the joyous images. "I've no idea who made it, but I'll be damned if it ain't of James and Sketch. Looks like he found his lass."

Sylvia stood still for just a moment. It was like she could hear laughter. The baby inside her gave a kick, and she smiled.

"Keep them both, they look much better here."

Acknowledgements

Writing a story about a masterful painter and the question of where our inspiration comes from was an idea that's been in the works for more years than I'll admit. As with so many people, *life* got in the way. From having two beautiful children, to the passing of my beloved mother, Debbie, sitting down to write just didn't take the priority. Much like Sebastian, I ran from writing. But there was no denying it, I am a writer. Eventually this writer, who cannot make a stick figure to save my life, listened to that inspiration to create an adventure out of art and see where that journey took me.

I want to say thank you to several people who have had a great influence on this story. I first want to thank my husband, Walter. He told me my idea was a good one when we were on one of our many road trips, which one I cannot remember now. I can, however, remember his words: "You going to write this one?" He's always been the one telling me to just go for it already. Thank you for listening to my wild ideas, then telling me which ones are good and which are not, for being the Artist in my life (and for helping me figure out those fight scenes).

Next, I want to thank A.M. Dunnewin, my dear friend for years now who talked me through some fantastical plots while sipping too much coffee. My writer-in-crime, as she has put it, has been the person who knows my struggles as a writer. Thank you for being an inspirational idea molder, my ruthless editor who leaves the best comments, and guide into the wilds of Indie Authorship.

I am also so very grateful to my family, especially my father Mark, and sister Heidi, as well as my friends, those who have encouraged me to write, especially when life of all sorts got in the way. Thank you for being there and for pushing me forward. Your love and support have sustained me through it all.

Last but not least, thank you readers. I wouldn't be publishing this book if it weren't for people taking a chance on Indie Authors. Thank you, and I hope you have enjoyed this adventure and had some fun along the way. That's the point, after all.

~GME

About the Author

Gina M. Engman grew up with a love of reading and began writing at a young age. She enjoys classic novels, fantasy and sci-fi stories, and loves the hero's journey. The rhythm of language, symbolism and hidden meanings drove her to become a writer. *The Mark of the Artist* is her debut novel.

When not writing, Gina enjoys road trips to the ocean, working in her vegetable garden, the Northern California sun, and sharing her life with her beloved husband and two amazing children.